Fragments
Unfinished Writings

Scott Shaw

Buddha Rose Publications

First Edition 2020

ISBN 10: 1-949251-28-4
ISBN 13: 978-1-949251-28-9

Library of Congress: 894668732

Printed in the United States of America
10 9 8 7 6 5 4 3 2

Fragments
Unfinished Writings

Table of Contents

Introduction

For anyone who has ever written literature, (or other stuff), you understand that though you may start many stories, you do not finish all of them. There's probably a million reasons for this but whatever that reason is, not all starts equal a finish.

Back in the '80s, with the dawning of the first generation of home computers, I was writing a lot of poetry, short stories, and novels. Many of those pieces found their way to publication. Though most of the stories and novels I started were completed, there were a few that just stopped. For whatever reasoning and/or logic I had at the time, I never finished them.

As the age of DOS and other early computer languages faded away, luckily I printed out all of those stories that were in various forms of completion. I printed them out on one of those noisy typewriter style printers. Maybe twenty years ago I had the idea that I should publish all of those partially finished tales just as they stood. Yes, I could probably go back into them and finish them if I wanted to, but then was then and now is now so it just seemed better that I did not go back into them as so much time had passed and so much in my life had changed. Up until this point in time I never got around to that task, however. I've been busy! Recently, I pulled out the folder that held those unfinished writings. Initially, I did an OCR scan of the first one I took out, Surgery of the Soul, and published it on my Blog. That got me inspired and I went through all of the other works in that folder and OCR'd all of them—leaving them in their pure and unadulterated form with no proofreading or updating.

Except for the few that have a date associated with them I cannot tell you the exact date each piece was created. But, they would all have had to have been written in the mid to later 1980s as before that I used pen to paper to create my writings and after that I moved onto Mac.

So, for the whatever it's worth, here they are, the foundation of several Scott Shaw novels that never found their way to completion.

Surgery of the Soul

By Scott Shaw, Ph.D.

To:
Denise and Judy
for all of the right reasons

To:
Xiao Ling and Li Fu, and Tiffany
for all of the wrong ones.

Chapter Uno

I ride through the rolling lush green hills of Southern China like a king in heat. I sit in the rear of a four-door sedan auto, dark blue in color, tinted windows in the back. I am accompanied by my bodyguard. In the front rides my driver, solo.

No, his name is not Solo; not like Napoleon Solo, like, you know, from the 60's T.V. series, *The Man From Uncle.* He just rides up front, solo. Name, well awh… Damn, that doesn't really mean that much now does it? He doesn't really play that much of an important roll in the tale I am about to spin anyway.

But, it was all like a dream; a fucking dream if you don't mind my using my native L.A. slang. Sooner or later slang always seems to become the norm, anyway.

The road passed in front of us. In front, soon to be in our rear. And, as the pagan green hills, covered with blooming life existed, dominating my field of vision, I was swept to dreams of the love that must be waiting for me here; lost into the dreams of all that this place holds for me, this Southern place/space.

China… Of ALL that it owed me, having been tossed out on my ear, psychologically and heart broken. What was it now, four years ago? But that was another tale, told in another book. And, the past, never repeats itself. Or does it?

I looked out across the green horizon; passing the so-called peasants working the fields; wearing large round, pointed topped hats, just like in the movies; realizing that it would have been a far better thing for China never to have opened the bamboo curtain at all, never to have tried to keep up with the modern western world; far better to have been alone, isolated, where the people would never have known the difference; lost to another glance in another chance.

As the castles of the former War Lords stood out and stared above the walls of civilization, in all of their ambivalent grayness; reminiscent of a different, a darker time, lost to it own suchness of nothingness. I was living a dream; and this dream that had to happen. I would not allow it to be any other way.

The passion stocked me. It forced its embrace upon me. Like the lips that had found mine, the day I left L.A. For out here on the outskirts, a million miles into the land of never-never, that too meant nothing. This is the place that held it all.

Green, the most mystical of colors, pounded my vision. The rice fields, where the people walked, planting their substance, the grey profoundness of the castles of power.

This was the land where Lao Tsu had walked. And now, it was mine; my playground.

As the warm Spring heat pounded onto the countryside surrounding me, engulfing me, even in some ways controlling me, I was lost to its omnipresence. I was contained, self-contained inside the dark blue auto in which I rode. I had a driver, a bodyguard, air conditioning, money in my pocket, a desire in my heart, and the green passive purity of passing pagan China, complete with its peasants outside of me, stroking my field of vision.

A car, a driver, a desire; her name Li Fu; Chinese, golden Southern China skin: a green card in one eye, a dollar sign in the other, but I did not care. I had seen those eyes before. Felt this desire one too many times to really care. I stared deep into myself, looking for a feeling, realizing that there should be one when there was not. I mean like, here I was on the other side of the world, other side of the world from where I was the week previous. I look, I studied, as the scenery passed, as the desires passed, as I wondered, knowing I should be feeling something, something more, something different, something about the here and the now; in a life that passes all too briefly. In studying, in looking, in the trying to care, I realized that there was nothing, that I felt nothing different, that I was nothing different. Nothing more than I was a week ago bound in L.A. Nothing more than I was years ago, when my feet were first placed upon this soil. God damn, like there must be something, but there was not. Just the passing green, a driver who didn't care; no not really, a body guard, only in it for the pay, for the prestige, a babe waiting hotel side, desirous of any *"gui-lo,"* (white boy) that may come along and show an interest. Who was the fool?

So, I guess I did it, gave you all of the specific in the first chapter, all of the games that would be played, all of the feelings that may be held, all of the nothing about to unfold. But, the games and the dance go on and on, and hey, like, all of this dancing does make a story. A story from HELL perhaps? A lot of times, life; it does look better, feel better, on words upon a page, of pictures upon a screen.

Read on...

"Doctor, I you don't mind, I need her over here, helping me with the surgery."

I almost told J.P., "Fuck you." and hit the brick. It was like I had asked the babe over to my position of surgery observation. She had just meandered her semi hot stuff my direction. And Doctor, I don't know, some how that term never fit me. Just call me X.

I don't know, out here on the hard road, you do find yourself in the strangest of position.

I had walked into the hospital the night before. I had gotten the *show me around.* I walked in, a major cockroach, whipped its bad self past me, crossing my path. The walls were dirty in this three-year-old building. Painfully white, as they attempted to hide themselves, in darker shades of dirty gray. People slept in beds or walked the halls in blue stripped prison looking uniforms. Their bathroom, tiled holes cared in the seven story floors. I.V. bottles hang from coat hangers, family, sleeping on the floor. Hard to believe that I stood there, in the late twentieth century in a modern kicking South China city with a forty-five story building standing next to it; modern, mirrored glass windows, outside elevators; international banking concern, owned and operated. You can see where their priorities are at.

Her name was Xiao Ling, this sweet little nurse who desired a diversion. I stood a full head and shoulders above her. But her eyes radiated the smile that was hidden behind the surgical masks that we all wore.

"You will perform surgery today. Dr. X?"
"No, I am not that kind of a doctor."

Damned, if I would ever want to be in actuality. I mean like all the blood, guts, the ectera-a-mundo. I don't know, sure it may be nice to help people. I mean like people do need helping; don't they? Awh, well hell, we are all going to die anyway.

The O.R. looked amazingly green on the inside. As the sun passed through the plastic flowered curtains which lung over the opened windows. Like, real sanitary, huh?

I never really planned for this journey. It just kinda happened.

Niederdorfstrasse

I was cruising down the Niederdorfstrasse in Zurich. I guess it could be somewhat compared to Melrose Avenue in L.A. or the Rue Du Faubourg area, over by the Pompidou in Paris. You know what I mean, sub-cultured, fashion passioned, new waved in the old wave sense, etcetera and so forth. Though certainly Zurich is not as big, not as busy, not as push'n full on as Paris, London, Tokyo, or L.A.

It was over by this little restaurant. I remember it well; in the winter, cold, the sign of the times. I was walking, I was wandering, lingering, considering to go in and have an afternoon bite to eat, when passing me on my left comes this sweet little young thing, candy bar in her hand.

The motion was movin', the steps set to pace. I had not really stopped, not really decided to eat; her pace met mine, "Hi," she said with a very thick accent.

Now from the looks of her, first glance and all, I placed her maybe thirteen, her hair brown, short, eyebrows thick, skin, caramel like the outer shades of the candy bar she was consuming. "Hello," I said, for what did I have too lose?

"Where are you from," came the obvious question.
"America," land of the free resounded in my mind.
"Are you looking for food?"
"No, maybe… I don't know. Why do you ask?"
"No reason."

Her voice spoke soft yet deep, her English good, yet accented. Eastern European I thought as we moved on down the street.

She had definitely attached herself to me. Me, being from the gutters of the city and the slums of the world, I wondered why.

She walked next to me making small talk. Me, I had no reason to run away. A sweet young child, my wallet safely buttoned in, talk is cheap, life even cheaper. For a moment or three, I thought that maybe she was a Gypsy. I kept my guard up.

Just a note, not being prejudice here or anything, but in Europe, well the Gypsy's do have a rather bad reputation. I'll leave it to the textbooks to explain that to you.

She told me that she had come from Russia, a soviet by birth and form, her accent led me to believe the words that she said, claiming that she wanted, "Freedom." And freedom is just another word for nothing left to lose.

"Where's your family," I asked.
"They're diplomats and I have the afternoons to myself. I like it here, don't you like it here?"

With that she said come with me. Into a candy store we walked, a candy store as we were passing by. I could see this young child's vices, I knew what lingered in her youthful mind. She ordered up two, of the newly processed poison, my mind thought, how nice, one for her, one for me. As it turned out, she said, "These are for later," and stashed them both away. So much for the generosity of a child.

We walked on into the cold of the day. I wore my long tan verging on the brown, shin length coat, a little piece I had picked up in San Francisco a time before. I love the winters when you can get all bundled up, a lot of clothing, long coats and the etcetera.

She, Sonia, my new little friend wore more of the fast and casual, 'let's go skiing,' kind of look. A short blue, lined jacket, a scarf, and a pair of American jeans.

She stood maybe to my shoulder, couldn't have been much taller than that. We walked, we talked, I even tried to get away from my apparent magnetic force with her but she held on tight.

Finally, with no possibilities of a solitary lunch, with haveable women and their possibilities in mind, I decided to go back to my hotel not too far away and sit back for a little afternoon nap. This was fine with her, for she wanted to go too. I could not believe her naiveté that she was wanting to go to a traveler's hotel room. I chilled the response in the winter chilling cold. Told her that I probably would see her later, see her again, as I would be here for awhile.

Though it took some doing, I finally had gotten away from her. Back over at my hotel, a little three star place that I like in Zurich, it is walkable, two blocks or so from the central train drop that goes right to the airport, or to other places and planes in Europe thereabout. Walkable so no taxi needable, keep life simple, you know what I mean.

Back in my room, I laughed a bit at the situation, wrote a bad description there of in my journal, had a brew, from the rooms wet bar, a chocolate chaser, seeing how my little friend had not offered me one and this being Switzerland and all. Then it was out, I was out; goodbye, gone to never-never-land. She and dreams the nap of the day, time to recoup, renovate for the nights and the maybes of what is to come.

No dreams spoke to me, not such as they were, no dreams that I can remember, awoke far too soon, far too fast.

"What are you doing here? How'd you get in?"
"The deskman gave me the key," she said, accent and all.

Initial pissed off, initial concern, who was he to give people the key to my room, I was going to have to have a talk with him.

"Did I wake you up?"
"Yes, but I guess that's OK."

Laid out into the forbidden realms, were anything can go and usually does. Sleep and all of it elation, lack of frustration, I had laid out in this really nice, really big, almost reclining three star hotel room chair.

Sleep and interrupt, I wondered what she wanted, this sweet young child with me. I told her the name of my hotel, that was a mistake. A mistake I had made before.

You know that it is almost funny, for long ago I have/had learned, don't tell people were you're cribin', they show up, want to have dinner, want to have lunch, want to hang out, want to introduce you to their sister; Southeast Asia being the pinnacle of this forced introduction form. But here she was, a little child, a child so I though, who would have thought that she would come a' knock, well an-opening, room numbered key in hand. Previously purchased absent from he chocolate bars, I guess eaten as the day had passed.

"What are you doing here," I asked.
"I don't have to be home until seven o'clock. That's when my mommy and poppy come back, so I like to look for things to do until then."

Now, I was feeling not too cool, latched up in the love shack with this young little child and all. I was about to suggest that we go out and have dinner when...

"I have to go to the bathroom."
"Right in there," I point.

I could not help but wonder how her parents could let her run around. I mean, I know, I was a street kid, gangs and all, but I am a dude and that was L.A. I would never let my daughter hit the streets.

Time passes, it seemed to take a long time, abstract thoughts and visions come to mind. Abstract in reality, abstract in form, can I tell a story, a story that was lived. Should I put it in parables, semicolon in hand, can I write it straight, in fear of judgment, well, let me be the party man that I am.

Out she comes, now the best way to say this, well... Is there a best way to put this? She was wearing my white hotel supplied bathrobe. White and the caramel of her skin, white and the night, colors they merge, colors they blend, it was not tied, slightly open in the front, down the center, I saw what she had, all the caramel colored passion of it.

"What are you doing!" I kind of jumped up from the daze in my chair.
"I am doing nothing, what are you doing?"

She walked closer to me. Now, let all things be as they may, I do love passion to the max, but call me a closet moralist, a republican waiting to come out, and though there was this one time in the Philippines; I mean, she was a bit young but...

She moved up to me, close to me, next to me, put her arms around me tight. I tired to move from her, push from her, dance from her, I tired but I did not try hard enough.

"It is OK, don't worry, I like you, I like you a lot."
"But I am an old man and you are so young."
"Thirty is not old."
"How old are you?"
"Never mind."

With that she takes my hand, willing or unwilling still I remember the question in my mind. She placed in between her legs. I could feel the soup was warm and full on.

She stood up on her toes, kissed me on the lips, I mean no questions asked, her tongue was down my throat. The kiss set my hand to motion, how could I do anything but follow my sword into battle. I massaged the beaver, a pussy with so few hairs, she controlled the situation but I came along for the ride.

She led me over to the bed, lay down upon the gold colored bed spread. Gold trimming the white, white accenting the caramel, give me a ticket, give me a ride, let me know the mastery, let me know the dark side.

I moved my hand up to her breast, so small, so firm. This was all like a junior high school kid's fantasy, and here it was offered, here and to me.

Now, call me a pervert, yes, well I probably am. Call me unrestrained, a moral degenerate, a cradle robber, etc., etc. Yeah, you can call me anything, but I tell you, placed that kind of available action in my hand, and well, that hand had to be played.

I moved and grooved for a time, as she was, like the perfect pro taking off my clothes. The kissing it was oh so fine, her body tight, firm, little, small, young. The thought did cross my mind more than thirty or forty times, a line for the Jim Croce song, "Five short minutes in heaven cost me twenty long years in jail," jail bait on the serious side and all. But my pup up, it didn't meet any resistance when she put it in.

I stroked and choked for awhile, then I rolled her on top, she had moves way superior of her apparent age. Me, back on the flip side, I played it oh so fine. Her pussy tight, like only a youngsters can be, her body, her movements, her kisses anything but the young and/or the untrained.

She gave the notion, I gave the motion, she came, so I blew it off.

"Did you like it?"
"I loved it," was my answer.
"We'll have to do it again," she said with a smile.

She grabbed me by the arm, pulled me into the shower, one of those hand on the wall inside the shower glass doors, kind and all. She washed me as I stood there in all that perpetual post cum realizations, questioning, "Why do I do this kind of stuff?"

I watched her young body, wash mine. The movement of the water flowing into the movement of time. I too was once her age, so much older now.

We finished up, it was approaching the seven o'clock hour. I inquired as to the fact of her impending having to be home. She said she was hungry and wanted to know if I would like to eat first.

First and foremost, a stitch in time saves nine, get this jail bait out of my room. How long will it be until my cum in her has dried up?

Out we go and into the early evening, I placed the key(s) at the desk. Just a smile from the deskman, I would save the talk with him until another time.

Didn't want to bring attention to myself you know what I mean.

Had he notice, he hadn't initially, but our hairs they both showed the signs of recent water emergence from being wet. The old, 'she is mine,' game; outside your babe and you strutting with wet do's. But this time it was different, for her, she was a child. Hiding would have been preferred, or the next plane out-a-Dodge.

I grabbed a taxi as it motored on by, in we get, in we go, a little, secluded place that I know.

Dark in the distance, the sun it had gone down, the sound of resistance, it is the last thing that I heard.

The streets in Zurich, they move none to fast, motor driven insanity, does not often take its toll. Smash bang, I saw it coming, I wanted to yell at the driver, in a intersection over by the lake, I saw the black car coming, I saw the black car turning, I saw the taxi driver, not seeing the lights, smash, I was out-a-there.

I woke up in this pale blue hospital emergency room with this doctor laying some smelling salts under my nose. Try waking up to that sometime, no fun in the maximum way.

I had a killer head ache, they said basically I was AOK, wanted to keep me for a day or three, just to check me out, my head getting minorly smashed and all.

"How's my friend," I inquired, she was all right, far better than I. The driver he got dupped up, head in the window, a thousand stitches or something, but he would live as well.

"Did I want to sue the taxi company," an inquiring lawyer wanted to know. They got the shysters everywhere; I just want to get out of here.

Now it was more than just a passing thought what my young friend had said or done. How long had I been down, what time was it now, hospitals they like to keep these things under wraps.

I sat in my now, semi private, hospitable sweet of a room, trying to get an objective on what was happening, trying to make my head stop pounding, neither/either seem do able.

It was later, how much later, I really did not know. The spins in all of the melancholy, the moments go in trying to grab hold. In comes the doctor, "How do you feel? He pulls the dividing curtain closed, wants to have a little talk with me. The shit was about to fly, my heart went thump, thump, thump.

"How well do you know that young girl you were with?" His eyes they stare deeply, accusingly into mine.
"Not well at all, why?"
"Did you know that she had multiply sexual partners today?"
"No, what are you taking about? Where is she now?"
"Where she is, I do not know, as soon as I finished examining her she left without anyone knowing."

I felt a sigh of relief.

"As I was examining her, I realized that it looked as if she had sexual contact today when I asked her she said it was with several men."

Wouldn't you know it, I though. All the sluts, all the whores, they always find their way to me. They look so pure, the promise of passion and all it ever was, all it ever good be, was a game for a price, a price I always had to pay.

22

He wanted to compare my love potion juice with what they had found previously, I told him to take a serious chill pill in that direction, he would not find anything anyway. I just had met her, I was just sharing a taxi, I thought that she was the child of a Russian ambassador, diplomat, or something.

"Russian, with an English accent," he asked.

Well fuck me again.

I know I had better get out of there, exit stage left and all. I wondered if my California medical insurance would cover this anyway and fuck doctor bills in Switzerland.

My head pounding, my heart pounding, I got my clothing, I got dresses. I realized that my leg had caught a shot, I had a bit of a limp, soon enough it would go away.

No one looking, over to one side, slide me out the soft cool way. I hadn't signed anything, from my drivers license they could have gotten my name but all being all, I was free and clear.

I grabbed a taxi, over to the side, I was actually none to happy about the whole taxi thing, I had left some stuff, my cameras, lens, and film over at this local guy's house that I knew. Thought that I had better get that first.

He lived in this house, a nice house, two stories on the hill and all. A family, mom and dad, and this guy that I knew, my age, but like he lived there at home with his parents.

In I go, my cameras to get, "Where are they?' "Here or there," was the answerer I was given.

Well fuck this or that, here or there, where be they be? Upstairs, on the table, one my main one, that bad boy had a thousand dollar price tag plus. Jon, the dude I knew, trying to be knowledgeable and cool, impress the women, depress the shutter, outside, he forgot it, last night it had rained and snowed. There lay my camera, a wet and tattered piece of shit.

I had more than a few words to say to this so called friend, who claimed he didn't feel it was his duty to pay the bill for the repair, "Well fuck you too than," I was out, the taxi waiting, to my hotel I was ready, my cameras, the ones that still worked, the ones that didn't, and I.

As I pulled up, as I paid the guy off, out of the black taxi I got. There in the distance, there to my left, blue sedan, my friend, young and of the night. She was in a car, driven by some grey old dude. I looked at her, she looked at me, I walked in that direction, they just drove away.

"Oh, your sister was just here looking for you," the desk dude says.
"What!"
"She went to your room to see if you were there."
"She's not my sister, did you give her the key?"
"Yes, but..."
"Couldn't you tell that we spoke different English?"
"No, she spoke American just like you."

Fuck me, again.

Up to my room, yes she had been there, yes my stuff had been gone through. The perfect alibi to my little linguist, Russian, English, American, how could you turn a child that you had sex with in? My clothing was intact, my possessions AOK, I guess it was karamicly good that my cameras had been left elsewhere even though there was a price to pay for their bing left. She had snagged onto some of my travelers checks, but I had the most of them stashed in the whereabouts well hidden and whereabouts unfound.

Yeah, they were American Express anyway, no problem in getting them replaced. She would have a problem cashing to get her monies worth though.

Down to the desk, I made some complaints; paid my bill, walked to the train station, train to the, 'flugenhaven,' airport if you will. 10:23 arrival
time, 10:55 plane to Paris. Out-a-dodge, fast.

So for what it's worth and the way things never seem. For is, what we dream of, the chances we take, the destiny we forsake, whatever the fuck anything is anything worth anyway? For all the love that is known and lost and the prices that have been paid that are too high, run away, run away.

Paris, where the lights are richer, the whores more obvious, and the nights are mine to own.

88.15.11

A Day on the Town

7:44 A.M., a quite ungodly hour to say the least. I was awoken, not by an alarm, the alarm in fact was set to radiate in one minutes time. No I was not awoken by that but just simply I awoke. Perhaps it was my biological, psycho/spiritual clock going off one minute before its appointed time, or perhaps not.

She lay there next to me, my sweet little Chinese American via Taiwan princess, (M.S.L.C.A.V.T.P.) She lay there asleep. In all her Asian brilliance. She is so beautiful as she sleeps. The only problem is that the majority of our time together we are physically awake.

It was for her that my alarm was set, certainly not I. I, me, well alarms suck and I refuse to live in and of a world were I must be awoke by them. She, (M.S.L.C.A.V.T.P.) was the one for which in was set.

Now it is not that I have not offered her a mystics daydream, a mystics illusion but fame and fortune and the stroking of the ego and all that kind of nonsense seemed to pull her out for she had been offered the position of fashion consultant on this soon to be up and coming low budget Hollywood movie. Complete with her name in the subtitles announcing it to the world.

As I stare into the red digital light emanating from my electric time piece, (never a wind up clock, I hate ticking.) My mind realize that it would be of sound and selfish judgment to turn off the alarm before it has the opportunity to go off, awaking her, (M.S.L.C.A.V.T.P.) from her sound and nearly unawakeable sleep.

27

You see she is one of those that can have telephones ringing in her ear, doors being pounded on, garbage trucks distilling the trash receptacles outside, even her body being made love to and she will not under any circumstance awake, her loss. So why not disengage the alarm which would make its attempt at her awakening to the sounds of the radio station dance beat thus giving us the opportunity to have a mystical breakfast and spend the day as we did the weeks before, that is until she took her current position on the movie set. Having breakfasts, lunch, dinners, afternoon teas, sitting in our cars discussing what we should do, which equals doing nothing next. Something she claims it is boring, something I claim it is dreaming. So turn off the alarm, why not? A chance once again dream.

As I reached to turn off the impending dance beat sound, about to trigger from the red digital light reaching its mark, (I have always preferred blue or green digital light, I have meant to buy a new bedroom clock, I must do that, but do not tell that to my current time piece until I do.)

"What time is it?"

I could not believe it she had awoken. Well maybe I could you see, she is one of those get up at 7:00 A.M. sort of people, claiming it is just the way she is. I don't buy that, one is what they make themself and what they choose to be.

"I guess its time for you to go to work."

Now I am generally much more grumpy, should I say at such an early hour. That is unless I am greeting it from the other side of midnight. But we had retired at unbelievably about ten-thirty last evening. That was of course post a serious session with the margaritas at a little Mexican food restaurant I know and only three hours sleep the night before. That was in no part due to our, hers and me staying up until my usual time schedule of retiring about four, four-thirty A.M. But then that was at her uck West Hollywood place and I was more that rudely awoken by cars starting, garbage being collected, and her very winey dog who I require to be in the bathroom on the nights I inhabit her abode scratching and yelping at the door.

28

Anyway back to today…

Now I guess we had put in our eight hours, ten plus in more my speed but at any rate she climbed over me, she sleeping closest to my window which faces the sea. Out of bed she got up and into and onto my bathroom sink. She headed to place make up upon her face, lipstick upon her lips, all of which she does not need. Now I am not saying it is not attractive and the bright red coating which she places upon her very voluptuous lips does not turn a dude on. Some faces just somehow do not need it, the make-up that is. It's just not necessary. She however never believes my words and feels quite naked without it, perhaps it is like I without my earrings.

As she prepared herself, I opened the drapes and watched the surfers out on the ocean making love to the winter waves. It is January now, though the weather has been quite unseasonable warm, much to my disgruntledness, none the less the winter waves were cranking and the early morning surfers were out in full splendor.

I sat there describing the activities of said surfers. Describing how this one unlucky wave warrior had just had a guy come down left and introduce his board into the opponent's face.

"Just like watching the Wide World of Sports," she exclaims as she has completed her function of getting made up and walking over and sitting with me on the bed.

"Why were you so icky last night," she asked. I immediately knew the words were spoken in reference to my being none too interested in making love well into the bounds of sleep with her hand on my erected crotch last evening. I so eloquently explained to her that simply it was due to the fact that she was just wangin' my weenie and getting me up which was not the essence of sensuality something which she knows very little about. Which is a sad and somewhat a very descriptive statement considering the fact of the immense amount of lovers she has had.

Now you know I am certainly not adverse to having those intimate late night love sessions and I do admit there has been more that a time or thirty when I have unsheathed the sword and given it to one of my sleeping little temporary consorts but somehow over the past month and a half, the time she, (M.S.L.C.A.V.T.P.) and I have been together, her level of fucking has increased but she just does not seem to have the talent for passion, something quite different from fucking and though she is to date the only one I have been unable to teach it to it has left me in a somewhat disinterested state with her sexually speaking. I mean you can only fuck so many times…

I explained that simply the pup rising to the occasion was not at all the definition of making me, 'in the mood,' so to speak and that if she wants to party there are a lot of other areas of my body that she can touch and late night movements she can make. Getting my dick hard is easy. Fucking is easy. But sometimes there needs to be something more.

With that discussion and explanation out of the way, I suggested that she bail work for the day and go and have a very special breakfast with me at this new place I discovered. She declined saying all the general and foolish excuses of responsibility and commitments, appointments to keep, etc., etc., etc.

"Just dream," I told her.

But unfortunately she does not have the temperament of much of a dreamer. Such a waste.

We spoke of all the things, she apparently likes to speak of, i.e.: when will we live together? When will we marry? How can she just walk away from a job? Not much of a dreamer, huh?

As we rose from bed and made our way towards my front door she questioned me as to the date of our departure for Asia. Now let me explain the particulars here. I thought she was a dreamer, so I invited her to come to Asia with me. Something which I have never before done. Maybe I was drunk, maybe it was a rap I do not really know. Maybe it was needing a dream of my own and she seemed to fit the bill; beautiful, more than beautiful, the woman I have painted a thousand painting of, before I ever even met her dressed in pure West Hollywood Glam Slam style, a vocabulary, hard to find in today's world. It must have come from her working for a newspaper for three years, anyway I made the comment, she took the bait. We should have left then and have let the illusion fall apart over there in the land of her birth. Instead we did not immediately go, we remained and spun through the holiday season. My illusion faded, my promises however continued. She got a job last week, something a dreamer never does, I have searched for a way out ever since.

My words continued of let's spend the day together, do what dreamers do; nothing. She, she had a 9:00 A.M. appointment. I was happy she would now be officially late.

"I'll never work in this town again," she exclaimed.
"Good, then maybe you can learn to dream."

Up to the point of our meting and subsequent interaction she was one of those chase the illusion kind of people. Giving up a job at a newspaper to work as a freelance illustrator, whenever the jobs may call, and design clothing, with hopes of having her own line.

Now I wish people like that the best and I am sure her, it all her self-describe self-forms, "I'm cute and popular." could in fact make their way by sexual means or otherwise to the top. In fact look she had already landed a $500.00 a week before taxes job on a low budget soon to be released Hollywood film. But that is all well and good and I wish people like that the best but please do not step into the world of a dreamer and expect there to be no friction.

"We can be together this Saturday. I have it all planned. But you'll have to pay."
"Thanks a lot, glad you could schedule me in," I replied.

With the ridiculousness of that statement we went into our rehearsed discussion and further exchanges of the waste of time of the material world and how all life leads to the same jobs described by a different name which ultimately adds up to nothing. But I understand ego.

"You're going to do something really flakey, I just know it," she proclaims.
"You're right, that is inevitable."

Now the discussion went on for a few more, but it seems so meaningless and I am sure you are becoming bored with the details so she went out the door, down the hall muttering something to the effect that I was stupid not giving her my new telephone number which I had changed yesterday.

Back to sleep seemed to be the order of business on the grill. To sleep I went. Maybe an hour or so later I awoke dragged my-self out of bed with decision full-on for a day on the town.

Choices

Why do we make the choices that we make, it has always intrigued me? Life is lived by availability. Yes, I know, I have long known but it goes deeper than that. Sure we could get into the psychological ramification of any given subject or choice but psychology often times seems to be the excuse of the rich, the educated, the psycho killers, though no doubt it does play a part.

What I am discussing here is why do we, the ones here in life, continue to make compromises, settle for second best, simply as a means to fill time, to not be alone, etcetera and so on.

No answers really, just philosophies, that frost a cake which has already been frosted as all philosophies do.

Me, I love the outside, it calls me out but when you play in the outside, well, it does have the tendency to hit back, case in point...

Now, need I say it, I am again involved with this babe that I really would choose not to be involved with, that is to say I would consciously choose not to be involved with. That is not to say that she is not far more than beautiful and/or not to mention that her body is not in full on babe shape, or her sex pedal to the metal, full on passion, but consciously here I am again, no where with a person that the price to be with is far higher than the reciprocation of any love, lust, presence, etc.

Same old story, huh? Seems like I have told it one hundred or more times before.

If I can jump ahead of myself just a bit here, to the night, last night, the day previous of which this text is being put to form. Again I sat there, Sunday night watching this show in Japanese, 8:00 PM Pacific Standard Time. Ninja, it is about ninjas, like the old west to those of a distant land, I watched as I do, when I am home, when I remember, I listen in the tongue of Nehongo. I listen, watch then I cry, cry as I do ever Sunday, every Sunday that I am alone, cry for that perfection of physical form, unknown, cry for that body of virgin physical, unknown, cry for the purpose, unknown. Well, enough for a fool and his tears. Back to the previous.

She shows up, up in her fashion passion style, up and onto the babe, namely me, the style jockey that she supposedly loves, sooooo muuuuccccchhhhh. She's Chinese. Chinese via Taiwan via the OC, then to West Hollywood, where she has thrived.

As evening goes, it went, again my plastic money, the green kind, I do not have, pays for dinner, expensive dinner, again, I am behind the wheel, again I being told that it is all her doing. I guess what I am trying

Coriander Shades of Tibet Tears

The scene was my first memory. It was my first memory and it is my last. The mountains they are old; old and weathered, ten million years of erosion of the ancients. A river it is flowing through the center of the valley, the valley surrounded by the ancient mountains. The fields around the river are green and yellow, fertilized by manual means for the mountains in all their ancientness have little left to offer the crops in forms of sedimentary nutrition.

The river, it is flowing, the sky is crystal blue, a cloud pats its hand upon the face of the mystical blue air that inhabits all space. It is warm, it is mid summer, yet atop the mountains still remains hints of snow, signs of glaciers too old to ever be forgotten in this modern world.

In the river play naked boys, naked boys tending to a naked beast, a water buffalo high in this mountain air.

I, well I, am on a road, a paved road, two lanes, one in, one out. In to Lhasa, out to the mountains. The mountains where the mystics and the monks once searched for nirvana, caving themself in a world already far too dense, caving themself to hide from the outside, hide from themselves. That was long ago, at least twenty-eight years ago; 1959 in all came tumbling down.

Now, 1987, there is roads I know for I was on one of them, roads linking directly the dominant power, the aggressors, the predecessors, the winner in the battle of soul, self, and acquisition, another toy in the pocket of the Peoples Republic of China. Yes, I was on their road. I was riding one of their bicycles; rented from a resettled mainland born Chinese, not Tibetan.

I rode on the road out, to find what was left of Shangri-La, to find what was left of mysticism, not only mine, but that of the land, the land know in English as Tibet.

The scene was my first memory, it was my first memory and it is my last. It was so different from what I had long expected, so different from what my mind thought it would see. But conception seems the cause of all falling from grace, so I allowed myself simply to see what I saw.

Daylight

Daylight it was about to break outside. The heat is was pounding/pulverizing, no air blew in through the open window to my right side.

It was beyond the time when I could sleep, perpetual jet lag haunted me like a fierce spirit screaming in my soul. A lady she lay next to me, I could hear her soft sleeping breath breathe, the only sound that could be heard shattering the enormous silence of this Southeast Asian morning.

The white sleets pined tightly against her exposed skin; golden and Chinese, it glistened with the passion that only this corner of the world could offer. I moved slowly, as not to awaken her, turned from the hypnotic spell which had held my eyes to her petite feminine form. I saw a lizard hanging tight, upside down onto the ceiling above and I could not help but wonder what purpose it had in choosing to live its life that way or what purpose human life had, I had, this night of love had. All questions in the mind of an in-motion American mystic dancing in a foreign land.

I almost wanted to go to sleep just to forget, just to dream another dream than this one I was apparently actually living but the heat, the coming dawn, the wonderment all held me bound.

It has been about one year, since that day as I sit here in Southern California, the ocean crying outside and I am no more the better for the love felt, the love left, and certainly not for the confusion of purpose which has left me sitting here in this summer afternoon alone. Not unlike the lizard who hung from that ceiling, I have chosen to walk a less formatted path. In doing so, like all of the dreamers of ages past I find myself generally overwhelmed by the illusion that the majority of all people find so much meaning in.

That morning, cars began to start and move outside, in this residential suburban district of Petaling Jaya, just outside of Kuala Lumpur. 7:30AM the alarm clock went off. She turned and kissed me and dragged her self from bed into the bathroom to shower.

"Would you like me to join you?"
"No, you remain here and rest."

I watched as her form faded behind the closing door, the water turned on as she prepared for another day at the office.

I knew she must have been tired, for we did not leave the disco where we had meet until almost 2:00 AM. Then we had gone up to the toughly air conditioned room of which I occupied in the five star hotel above. A hug led to a kiss, a kiss lead to a touch,

"I guess that we are going to stay here," she said.

But I was in the mood for some diversion other than the basic, take them upstairs, western style, to my abode which rose thirty-eight stories in the sky. I lifted myself from atop her body,

"No, lets go to your place as we had planned."

As the story goes, later told to me, she had been latched up with an in-house love stud for a year or three, he had recently dumped her, moving out and on and now it was time to play. Me, I was the lucky one to get to be the indroduc-er to the night/the manufacturer of the dream; the first quai-lo, (white person) which she was ever to be with.

Small and pretty, her eyes found their way onto me as I left the dance floor with an East India local who in no way had the moves to be a-dancing with this kid here. Those pasted eyes, never left me. Nor, did her smile throughout the evening, as we spoke, as we danced. At times it almost annoyed me, I would be throwing a cruel move onto the pounding disco beat, look up and she would be full on eyes, full on smile, attired in her white pants and top; typical Southeast Asian garb.

The days in Southeast Asia, well they just didn't seem to hold too much illusion, too much panic, too much of anything at all for me anymore. It is like there comes a point when you have been there for so long and so many times that it just doesn't phase you anymore. I mean you can only see so many impoverished people to realize that there is no hope for this world at all and you can only view the affluent driving their Mercedes through the ransacked streets so many times before it just has no effect.

Especially in a place, a big city, like Kuala Lumpur. It is modern and from this its massive poverty is not so blatant. It does not hold all of the massive culture, complete with the temples to prove of its existence, like say in Thailand, Burma, or the like. It had just come to the point where I didn't even feel like going outside in the pumping Southeast Asia daytime heat anymore. I had taken thousands of photographs of far more desirable things than shopping malls, retail establishments, Rolex dealerships, and cars that go bump in the day.

So, they just passed; the days, like here in L.A. Today, yesterday, the day before that… I don't know, it is a funny thing/a funny feeling, like you try to think up things to do but what has any meaning?

Today is Monday, that day a year back, I really do not remember; yes, now as I think of it, it was a Thursday, into a Friday. The flow of the never-ending tick tocking of time. Our only salvation for certainly of what is the reason of the life going on forever like this. I guess the people that have a position, a job, this girl; yes Seow Yen, she had one. I suppose it makes one feel like they belong. Belong to what/for what, is the only question. A hundred years of employment adds up to a life with no room for creativity. I don't know, I guess most people aren't all that creative anyway. I was always the black sheep of the family, not that my family was very large. But the one who was destine to dream and do all the nothing which makes

Dogs in Heat and Meaningless Massacres

1

I got lost in the suburbs of another woman. She was not hard to find. I walked in any direction from the main direction; you know the one, love, faithfulness, forever, all that bullshit that doesn't exist anyway.

The main squeeze, I was departing, was like a knot in my soul, my hands bound behind my back. Once; yes, once-upon-a-time, I had believed the lie, I had bought into it with a gambler's bank roll. But no matter how good things are, they always get old, and the babes, they only do the LOVE action(s) for a few months at best. Central, and the central city love, I walked into the arms of anything that was available. Availability, it is not hard to find, if you are not too choosy, and if your eyes are wide open. I was not and they were.

Inner city sub warp streets, they were swarming, I walked them, post the LUST encounter. The pale grey of the buildings rising into the sky were haunting and I, I moved alone. Grey, red brick, grey into the blue, in all of their anonymity they called out my name. The noise of the city hammered/pounded, the honking of the cars horns, the firing of the engines, the slam of the breaks, it was music to my ears. The colors, the buildings, and the sounds all formed themselves into a haze. Yes, a green haze, covering the miracles of modern man, concoctions of the mind.

I had no one I wanted to speak to, nothing I wanted to say. A lone drifter in the city of my birth. That was AOK, people don't have much to offer anyway; just lies and rap about whatever melodrama that they may be wound up in that moment. I was sick of it, didn't have time for it anymore. The female form of diversion had proved nothing to me, only a ticket out. The main squeeze, why even bother discussing it. It was all just A-typical male macho nothing, and a little girl trying to fight back with her best blows,

"I didn't love you anyway."
"Fuck that, who cares."

I don't know, I guess it has gone on through out eternity. Eternity, what a word. Me, I was stepping out; where, who knows?

The telephone rang, it was 11:59 in the PM.

"Why did you do that. Why did you tell me."

I just hung up. I looked around myself

2

Out on the outskirts, desire it is not hard to find. Desire is easy, fulfillment of that desire, well that is a different story. You can run away from it, desire that is. How far, is the question? It will always chase you. The needs of a man, the programming of society. I don't know, call it what you will, it does pursue.

I was shacked up at this bro of a soul boy's crib; a gas station. Pretty cool pad, if I may say so myself. The city, back there, my city, no, I probably would have had a problem of one sort or another living in such an abode. Ego, you know and all. But out here on the outskirts, I could always come up with an excuse, "Oh its not my place, I just stay here," etcetera and so on.

The setting well, the setting it was this little backwater truck stop that no trucks stopped at. You know the kind of place, where the welcome to, and the thank you for coming signs hang on the same signpost.

Actually, it was not that small of a little town but close.

It had eight or ten streets, a hundred or so people, all living back there in the how-you-say, some sort of past and wishing to move on and out to some better future that they know must be awaiting for them further on down that Southern Oregon Highway. Me, I was just passing through. Yeah, a passer by that knew what he had come from—had no idea where he was going; the syndrome of no place left to run.

So, I was motoring on through, going mobile. Oregon, it is not that it is not pretty in its own sort of way but somehow it is just that it is not, what should I say, grand, yeah, or something like that. Further up the coast, (that I was actually a hundred or so miles inland from the said ocean), is Washington. Somehow it all fells different up there. The trees, they are bigger, larger, or something. Maybe, more dense, yes, more dense. Oregon is like a want-a-be Washington, or a could have been California. Mostly it is just what it is. I will leave judgment aside.

The people, yeah the people on the other hand, especially the local-yokels are hicks to the fullest and though some try to be otherwise, they don't much dig outsiders, especially Californians. So, my ride, I had it placed backside of the station, a car cover upon it. Covering up my license plate, if you know what I mean.

As for Skip, my friend, newly found, and a bro; well, he was the soul bro, if you catch my meaning (soul/sole). How he got up there, well that I tell you later but he was how should I say, out of his element. Oregonites had there way of not liking anything too distant from their own lily white color, especially out here in the distant civilization suburbs, a million miles from the city.

Myself, having grown up in Watts and for more than a short time being the only white boy honky in my elementary school, color didn't have too much of an affect on me. At least not one that meant any more than the colors upon a canvas.

We understood each other, Skip and I. It was instantaneous. I cruised on into his station. He was asleep at the desk in an old and dirty white tiled office, separated from the world by glass. Feet upon the old wooden desk. Grey blue station shirt, greying hair. A face that could have been a punch drunk fighter, lines and scares. I pumped my gas, walked in, knocked on the desk, he opened his eyes, "Yeah, what do you want?" So, I paid him.

He sat up, stood up, pulled out a bottle of the Jack, you know Tennessee sipping whiskey, out of the desk drawer. And the rest, well the rest is history, or at least literature here upon these pages.

I was invited, no place better to be; I decided to stay for a day or two. Oregon not all that inviting but... There was an upstairs on the far side of the structure, over the garage and a trailer to the side. He cribbed the trailer, offered me a key and the upstairs.

It was a mess, just like my apartment back in L.A., so no problem. Divided into two rooms, the main one had a kitchen type set up: a sink, a stove that no longer worked, a refrigerator, that did. A table, a double bed. He and his once-upon-a-time wife had settled there. Settled there until she left him, better things a calling on down that road, you know. The trailer, somebody had left it parked, six years back, so he said, they never came to get it. Skip decided it was easier to live in there than to walk up the stairs.

Fugitive

fu-gi-tive (adj.) 1. Fleeing or having fled, as from pursuit, danger, arrest, etc. 2. Not fixed or lasting; transient. 3. Wandering; shifting. 4. Treating of subject of passing interest; occasional—n. One who or that which flees; a runaway or deserter.

$$*\qquad*\qquad*$$

fugitive
alone embraced by the one
one embraced by the alone
movement
a life in movement
movement to the nothingness
which equals the whole
illusion offers the mergence
illusion offers the dream
illusion offers everything
illusion is desire
desire is lost by the one
one is alone
alone is one
the one moves onto the everything
everything begins as nothing
nothing ends at everything
nothing and everything
everything and nothing
anything is the answer
the answer to not being alone
alone merges one
one merges to two
two equals desire
desire for one
desire for two
two is the everything
one is the nothing
one is movement to two
two is the movement to desire

one is alone
alone is movement
movement to the two
movement to desire
desire is movement
movement to more
alone is one
alone is movement
alone is fugitive
fugitive

*   *   *

I am a fugitive in my own land, my own city, my own space. I am a fugitive though I have done no crimes. I am a fugitive, I am alone.

Here I am a mystic, an artist, never employed; a dream to most. I look around my $910.00 a month apartment. There is rolled paintings to my side and over behind me against my kitchen bar. There are guitars and keyboards in my bedroom. A sadly rusting, high tech, easel is on my nighttime patio facing the ocean, outside. On my walls are thankas and images from Asia; purchases on my journeys around the world.

I sit here on Halloween night 1987, I am twenty nine years old, handsome by most standards, I am wearing expensive Italian made clothing, my hair is long, I need a shave as I generally do, and I am alone, very alone.

Perhaps this all sounds like a complaint made by one of those typically bitchy people. It however is not, it is simply a statement of fact.

Somewhere all the truth in the moment has become lost, somewhere out there on the realms where all psychological battles are fought. Somewhere, in the place where it has just become too old to listen to complains about all of your bills and the amount of your rent. The guilt laid on me since childhood has cut too deeply leaving scare tissue. The kind that hurts inside when you move.

The real man would say, "Go get a job." Somebody yelled that at me from a passing car once. I yelled back, "Go get enlightened." Yet, that no longer is enough. For in all my knowledge, all my degrees, all my experiences, I have no answers only confusion.

Through it; all life has remained life and the answers to the questions, to the problems have not shown themselves. Thus I remain in continual flux, movement.

Objects such as jobs, they are no longer valid to me. In them there is no purpose. Simply following the commandments of the slave driver to reach the ultimate goal, the mantra of desire, the $ sign. I use the U.S. $ sign for it seems all in their pagan foolishness wish to worship it with the bounds of this country; America.

This life that I have lead, though a dream to most, has left me here completely lost. Lost for I have seen too much, experienced too much, and known what is possible. It is possible, yet "It," in time will fade as well. Fade to nothing; not anything. For that is the only truth I may impart to you in these few beginning lines. That is through "It," no matter how great equals nothing, not anything.

Somewhere in all the nothingness it seems that there must be purpose. Not the fool's purpose; that of having a family and leading a family life. Or that of the remaining employed through out eternity, purpose. There must be a deeper purpose, a deeper meaning. Not that of those who sit in caves, monasteries, temples, or churches, believing they are holy either. For that is a fool's elixir. Somewhere something.

I though that the mystic life led to fulfillment. It does not. Enlightenment is easy. As it has been said before every fool has it in the palm of his or her hand. Once known, what comes next? It does not give one friends, in a world full of bullshit people. It does not give one money, unless one is not truly enlightened and simply turns their borrowed knowledge into the market place and with a loud voice develops a following. It does not remove all the psychological problems laid on one in their childhood and for that matter adulthood. It in fact leaves on even colder for the truth is seen and what illusion is left. My advice, keep your eyes closed. It is easier.

The bohemian, artistic, life that was supposes to be full of Bukowski's myth: love, lust, desire, a woman around every corner. But here I am having lived that life as well as the aforementioned for many years and I have had my pud in my hand more than it has been out of my pants.

My advice leave the poetry, the art, the music for the fool who wish to live a solitary life, or secondarily that of the business person who is no artist or bohemian at all, just another bullshit person, in a world full of bullshit people.

What should you do then, seeing how life has no meaning and the dream lifestyles leave one alone and empty? Well I don't really know but I can tell you how I got here which may prevent some of you from making the same mistake.

I was born in L.A. in the late fifties and grew up in the sixties and seventies, a turbulent time to say the least. My parents moved me around the L.A. area pre my tenth birthday, the year my father died, a lot, in their attempts to find a home comparable to their desires. My father used to say, by moving you make a lot of friends. This was obviously untrue for I have kept in touch with none of them and none have kept in touch with me. My life as a mystic began early. Early in terms of a young boy's interest and choice.

It is told to me that my father traveled to India during his tour of duty in "The Big One," World War II. If this is true or not I do not know. Now with him dead many years and all his immediate family gone as well, I have no way of knowing. If it proves to be the case, then perhaps some passing yogi labored a psychic connection onto him which transversed onto me. Who knows?

I first remember being consciously exposed to the term yoga when I was about five by this man who has made his fame and fortune teaching yoga on television and otherwise. I used to practice it with him as my teachers as I sat home a hatch key kid long before that term was coined. Then living with my mother in the Wilshire district of L.A. It was a book by the same man, I remember it saying that one should breath in deep expanding the stomach unlike most who breath shallow and contract the stomach upon in breaths. To this day I watch my breath and perceive its correctness.

Then when I was the age of thirteen, I went into a bookstore over on Western Avenue just North of Wilshire, it is not there anymore, where I saw this book, the Tao Te Ching. I was drawn to it immediately. I went home and explained its importance to my mother who gave me the money to return and purchase it. I did.

The same text is now placed on my massive bookshelves over my left shoulder. If my mother has done nothing else positive for me the purchasing of that text for me, on that evening so many years ago should relieve all her bad karma.

Is that where it all begin, my path as a mystic; perhaps, I do not know. It may have been just simply my destiny. Destiny, the word seems like such an excuse.

I read the book that evening, and have since read it literally hundreds of times. Perhaps I will take sometime and read it again now.

Though my spiritual path has been deeply involved, both in the physical and non-physical worlds, I have found no translation of the Tao Te Ching which compares to the one that I purchased so many years ago.

India

It was a rather warm late summers day in North Central India. I was motoring through the countryside, riding shotgun in this jeep. As this dude, a Brit by birth and characteristics was at the helm.

We rode along; the wind, it felt good, it altered the state of perspired, suchness that permeated every inch of ones body in South Asia.

Life on the Hard Road
Poetry from the Asian Extremities

1

it is funny how I am
I always desire to meet a girl
I never desire to meet men
I see myself
looking at women
and wondering...

I guess I came to India
for the wrong reasons
in fact
I don't know why I came

but anyway
here is where I am
when I was younger
I was so austere
but what did the vegetarianism
and karma yoga get me
(well, I guess it got me here)

but here I am
the same person
that I always was
I guess we always stay the same

I see yogis, swamis, sadhus,
beggars, and bums
I see them every day
once I walked among them
but now I don't see what their difference is
they say it is for a reason
once I believed that lie
they say it is for their next life
what next life

life,
we are living this one

Delhi, India 1982

anyway
on with the day
another day
what a day
and another day goes by

I get up early
I walk the streets
7:15 AM
I walk past
I walk over
the people street sleeping
this town it does smell bad

the India army men
faded uniforms
rank patches hardly sewn on
they choose to make a joke of me
speaking in their hindi tongue
I walk away
grab a scooter of a taxi
ride it
to the other side of town

it is like my feelings
moving from one side to the other
it is funny
how my feelings
they change so much
so often
in this place
one minute I hate it
the next, well it is not so bad
maybe it is just this city
I want to see the spirituality
the holy

not the city folk
dreaming of America
so I walk on
dance on
another day gone buy

Delhi, India 1982

3

to Connaught Place
New Delhi central
a sitar
and a view of the sitar factory
I thought that it was close
but no, it was quite far
a ride into the population
a ride through the closing doors
a ride with a lady
a sitar factory lady
too much traffic
too much pollution
we walked on

return to my dismal hotel room
I sit back
and play it for a time
I see how beautiful it is
how much work went into its construction
It was worth it
unlike most people
who just blow their money
it is something to hold on to

Delhi, India 1982

Manila

Out on the streets, it was early in the Manila morning. Out on the streets, I liked to call it observation, I liked to call it experience but the truth being told, I really had nothing better to do. The masses, dark skinned, almost Asian eyed, they were in the mode of travel, traveling to the office, to the work place, to the bread winning nowhere that this world seems to be all about. I walked among them, I dodged their cars as I crossed their streets, I moved, with no idea where I was moving to, just walking, in the pale overcast heat, that was developing in this semi-tropical climate.

Across my shoulder, I wore a bag, a bag full of cameras, heavy, I always took too many, carried too many. It gave me a feeling of purposefulness, when in fact I had none. None and nothing, I guess I was at home walking out there among the masses of those going somewhere to nothing.

I could not help but be overwhelmed by the shear impending massiveness of the weight, of the feeling, of the pounding of this culture going nowhere fast. The streets were filled, cars, pollution, people; it was maybe 7:00 AM.

I felt my pull, to what feels to me, the west, the left, I followed it for I had nowhere else to go. I walked, I walked on.

The heat was deadening, or the humidity maybe, something was deadly, there was definitely death in the air. The pale blue air, I saw it as that, I still see it as that. I looked to the sky, hazy blue grey clouds, life is hazy, I never did, never do know what to do.

My travels took me past a stadium, baseball, football, or otherwise, I do not really know, I guess I don't really care. How much do I really care about, how much do you really care about?

I think it was there, yes, it must have been, there where I got the first glimpse, glimpse of a time gone by, gone by state sides, gone by, but not too far gone here. Spray painted on a wall was a large A with a circle around it; anarchy, a punk slogan, from a punk time, 1977, 1978, even 1979, but not now, it must have been late 1986. Yes, November 1986.

It brought me back to another time, a time when I was far more young, far more idealistic, far less tainted, yet never so foolish to believe that anarchy held any answers. Well, at least not any answers for me.

Yeah, I was a punk, back then, the 70's, when it seemed to hold an alternative, a new reason, a secondary chance at freedom on a bourgeois scale. Mysticism my practice, anything but nothing my reason.

I danced within its limitless bounds for a time, a time until it became far to commercial, far too employed, far to used as a method of nonsensical violence, for the macho wanta-be jock fools of the world.

That was a long time ago though, a long time perhaps in chronologic sense, not in the sense of the heart. I guess once you are something there is the tendency, when it was good to you, to hold onto the memory, believe in the reason of it.

It was hot, the morning sweat rolled down my face, I pushed it back, pushed it back through my hair, I realized almost laughingly that I, yes I, Mr. Long Hair, once again had short cropped hair, the kind I used to wear back than, back when I was a punk. Tight short, standing up straight on top. God, I hate(d) short hair.

Somewhere, somehow, some fool streak in me a month before, back in L.A. had gotten this way stupid notion that I was getting too old to have long hair anymore, so I went for the cut, first to this dude, highly recommended named Randy out in San Pedro, he mega fucked up the cut, and when I asked him to just wack it and make it shorter he got temperamentally pissed and booked the shop. Than on and back to my main, via Japan, hair stylus this way nice X-junky of a still seriously ready to party sort of chick, she cleaned it up, I kept giving her the, "shorter, shorter." "It's going to stand up." "That's, OK." Done and over more than a few tears shed, there I was in the Philippines, for the first time, short hair, way gelled, way punked, only one earring in my left ear, as opposed to my general several in both, had to keep it conservative, you know, looking at a circled A, anarchy, life, it is funny.

I walked on, deeper into the movement of the city, deeper in to the bowls of the city. The streets, they got less paved, more muddy. The houses, less constructed and more destructed.

What is it with me, somehow I always have this way of finding the worst areas of a place. I guess as they say, "You attract what you feel."

                    *   *   *

the smell of the streets
the smell of the day
that has risen from the dead
known only as the night
the kiss of the foreboding
the smell
yes, there is a smell
lost
defeated
desire for the difference
it permeates the air
it holds control
of the soul
crawl out
there is no other way
climb out

and be shot down
walk in it
breath of it
let it cover your body
it will take possession of your soul
known
it cannot be denied
felt
it cannot be forgotten
lived
there is no running away
no matter where you go
or how you try
the poison of the mud
the passion of the lost
the possession of the uninitiated
it becomes all that you are

*   *   *

I walked, a picture or two, when no one was looking, trying to keep the massive resale amount of the cameras in my bag less-known in this more than impoverished, obviously crime-ridden section in the heart of the wrong side of the tracks Manila.

Old broken down, rusted, dilapidated cars lined the side of the streets. Houses, were constructed from less than 'up-to-standard,' materials; pieces of sheet metal, cardboard, used and abused planks of wood. Laundry hung from the windows, pink, white, yellow, all the glorious bright colors of the Philippines. Mud, it was everywhere, it was the only. My new, New Balance tennis shoes, bit the dust as it were, or should I say, bit the mud. Cars, occasionally drove by, I chilled back to avoid the splashing mud. Eyes, when they saw me, were on me; this white, blond, and obviously out of place Westerner strutting the streets of the low side of town. If only they knew how much I fit in.

*   *   *

Travel guide, no, I am not trying to give you one. I moved on. Time, it was pushing 9:00 AM. I came upon a group of boys playing a little hoop, B-ball in the mud, a more than interesting concept. They young ones, they were digging my scene, the older ones, held the distaste of the years of Western, U.S. intervention, dominance, and the political genocide of the Marcos years, they didn't like what they saw. I knew it, they knew what they could do but they continued to play basketball, I took a casual picture or two, from lenses that would fog up due to the morning humidity the minute I would pull the lens cap off. Pull off the polarizer, the UV filter would fog up, pull of the UV, the lens itself would fog up.

Fog, a nice enough effect, I thought. Perhaps it would hide or contrast some of the hate in these people's hearts for the waning world around them.

I walked in the mud; the distance, the horizon, the large skyscraper structure of the new city, where all the bullshit business takes place could be seen. Cruel, I thought, the mud and the distant yuppie empire of concrete. It's always that way in city though. I wonder do the working masses look out and see, can they see, do they have the vision to see, do they give a damn, and have they ever walked the streets of this mud. God, those streets of mud, hard to forget.

To the right, the North, I guess, it called me, I walked to its calling. The mud it began to subside, it moved to its logical end, pavement took hold, cars were more prominent. The ones, that is, that were running, not some ones lost dream laying in plying leaps of rusting metal in the streets of mud.

People moved, dressed a bit better; but clothing, that is changeable, the feelings were different, not so intense, but than intensity is where I have always felt my best, performed my best.

Somehow everything looked white here; it was white, the buildings, the houses, the businesses. White, it always seems like it is hiding something.

The noise of the still relatively early morning city pounded in my ears. It was a strange beat, one it seems like I had known somewhere in some distant place before, yet, I could not grasps on to the exact location, the exact time, or place.

Cities, they all, they each have their rhythm, their own individual beat, pounding, the sound pounding, like a drum directly in the ear of the oblivious, most can never hear this rhythm, most never known its origin or form, most only live their lives never taking a second to see, to hear, beyond the world's facade and physical form, most just pass through life, though the Tao Te Ching say it is only one in three, me, I say it is nine and three quarters in ten. The sound, the beat, it pounds, it pounded in my ear, like it was for my ear, my ear and to hear, hear to here, here, I was, there I was in the middle of the beat.

Painted on a white walls, in the white section of the city, again A in a circle; anarchy in motion.

The Philippines, I thought, how perfect, now I began to understand, anarchy was in progress, more in progress here, now, and then, than it had ever been in the seventies in the U.K. or the U.S. Anarchy by any other name, anarchy just and still the same. I felt it...

I walked on, a photo for remembrance, a photo to show to some non-interested urban or cultural geography class that I probably would never teach, but I had been through so many, been in graduate school, I thought, maybe, well maybe... And, you never know.

It is all so non-descript, white buildings, a photo of the said, in the city, a city on the extremities of the earth, where the earth and time and culture collide, it was the same, think of white buildings, anywhere any place and you too are there. Me, I prefer the mud, for there, in those realms, there is art, art that is not known, art that they do not know is art, the art of slow, painful and casual destruction. Death every time, they move, move closer, move farther, no way in, no way out. I could smell it, I could hear it; the beat.

White here, the beat pounded on, but the middle class ruled the turf, art was gone, there is no art in the middle class. Art is from mud, art is from death. I walked on.

T.R., I saw it upon walls, I had seen it before, where? Encircled, it was painted clearly in the white, in the heat, I saw it five, ten, fifteen times. T.R., I saw it too, what was it.

Walking as I do, as I did, I mean what else is there to do? Out once you are out, there is nothing to do, but continue. It is like life; walking, yes, it is like life for there is so many times that you would just as soon prefer to sit back and watch for awhile, but like a ball; yes, like the basketball those Manila B-ball players were throwing, once it is in motion, its like you cannot, can never stop, until you're slam dunked and hammered into the ground somewhere.

I came up and upon a/this group, a group over in the white section of the city, they were amassing. Banners were in their hands, banners were in the air, written in English condemning this and damning that, mostly condemning the U.S. for having supported Marcos. Some of the group wore scarves across their faces, red scarfs, others yelled through megaphones organizational commands, political slogans.

U.S., I was U.S. but more behind what they/these people had to say then what was being said Stateside, for they were the ones who had lived through all the oppression, not us; us and the U.S. Nor was I worried about the impending verification that I was U.S., always out there on the hard road, people always think I'm German, I guess because I have blond hair. I actually don't have any German blood at all but it has kept me clean in a few dirty situations out on the extremities.

I sat, well stood back and took a few pho-to-graphs, for posterity, for that geography class, I will probably never teach. Let them think, I can tell them I am International press I thought; ego, ego, ego.

They marched off, me, I walked off, feeling all the better for the experience, I mean hey, I got to pho-to-graph, a real and for sure Manila demonstration.

The heat was coming down on me, as I headed in the direction of the massive structures of financial solicitude in the distant. There I thought I could get something to drink, my body had reached about the dehydration point for I was no longer sweating and it did, out there in the heat, out there in the street, begin to worry me more than a bit.

The sky was fading from the blue/grey overcast; overcast, yes, I like that word, to the pale blue-sky heat of equatorial island Asia.

The heat, it was pushing me. I could not push back. How can you push something you cannot see, you can only feel, as it pushes you in the depths of the taking hold of your soul.

I needed rest, I needed drink, I had none.

The buildings, in consistence and color were fading. I had entered almost a no-mans-land, between the city and the people and the structures, bold and condescending in the distance. No more encircled A's, no more T.R.

Yes! T.R. Totally Recked, (wrecked). It had been from a movie released in the States maybe two years back. It was a movie of punk kids lost and alone, all for various reasons of form finding themselves living together.

That was it. Here in Manila, they must have gotten the movie on the screen or via videotape, gotten it and related to it; punk, a reason, wrecked, the world. The world and a reason, life and a hard thing to find. I could understand where they were coming from.

I made it to Makati, this structured foreboding place. It was cold, cold in the heat, I did not like it there. I did not even find a place to catch a cold one. Up the street a bit, the heat putting me down, back around, I needed a taxi. I hate it in the heat, when it is whipping you down and there is nowhere to turn, nowhere to run, nowhere, nowhere. It has happened to me more than a few times.

Finally a taxi, finally a ride back to my hotel, finally…

We drove not so different, from the course I walked, veering to the left of the mud ridden streets of impending doom; doom and art, we drove in air-con'ed comfort while the world in its heat moved around us as we moved around it. The taxi it was yellow.

A wall, white, we passed it, T.R., yes I understand, the dream, the dream to dream, the no where, the no way to run and where can you go when there is no place left to go, we arrived at my five star hotel.

*   *   *

I took the elevator up to the top floor, past the floor man, strategically placed at a pulpit, white, facing the elevators,

"Good Morning Mr. Steve."
"No, that's Shanti, Steve is my first name."
"Oh, sorry Mr. Shanti, good morning."

Yeah, right. I opened the door, into the hall I went, I tried to find the bedroom, but took a wrong turn or three.

*   *   *

I had pulled in last night, the night before, my flight LAX to Osaka. Money a problem and traveling a necessity, I elected to not make my tradition gateway to Asia stop in TKO, Tokyo.

I had a couple hour late airplane from LAX layover in Osaka. I had never been in that airport before. Funky, way funky. I was way surprised for it being Japanese and all, and I mean hey, Narita is so nice. But, I chilled down a cup of the java, "Cohi dozo," my ego pumping that I could rap some of the lingo and wallowed in the feeling of why hadn't I lived here forever, fallen in love young, not become so worldly, messed up, and tainted and lived happily ever after with some sweet subservient Japanese princess.

Up in the air, out and through and onto Manila, taxi ride to the hotel in the pounding heat, a very serious faggot at the desk, you know the kind; looked like the original cocksucker, the one who invented it,

———
69

"Were sorry, all the rooms in the hotel are taken."

I was just about to get pissed for I did have a reservation.

"We'll have to give you the Presidential Suite. "

So faggot handed me the key and touched my hand a way I did not like at all, had I had a few in me I would probably have gone up side his head but the Presidential Suite and all and hey, I am a nice guy right.

The bellman looks at the key, the number on the same,

"Oh nice room."
"Yeah, I don't know, they are just giving it to me because all the other rooms are filled."

Into it, he walks me through and into the master bedroom area where my closet is to be found, unload the load, toss him a tip, he is out-a there. It was almost like a joke, I mean I am not one to go econo, but I walked my way through the place, it was about twelve rooms.

There was a conference room with a long power session table with twenty chairs, two living rooms, a dining room, three bedrooms, five T.V.'s, a kitchen full on, bathrooms with gold platted knobs, and a kill view of Manila, etectra-a-mundo. I mean, I had just moved into this newer single beach front apartment from a funky old beach one bedroom back in L.A. I mean, I laughed at myself, I laughed at the situation. See, I always had this idea that I was destiny for greatness, be it spiritual, musical, artistic, poetic, otherwise, or etcetera. I had however not gotten anywhere with anything. The truth and the world had begun to close in on me and here I was twenty eight years old, without a dime in the bank, owing the credit card companies plenty; anxiety, it was touching me. I mean what can I say, it was almost like a cosmic joke. I hated it, for I thought this is the way I should be living all the time but instead I was cribbed up in a small apartment tripping over my possessions. I had intended, I had thought that by twenty seven something would have happened, I would be there or at least on my way. I was twenty-eight, lost, confused, all alone, and without a clue as to what to do in life. I thought I would be somewhere but was nowhere.

Nowhere but here/there. Manila, another chance another dream.

*   *   *

I found the bedroom, tossed down my camera bag, walked around until I found the route into the main living room and pulled me a cold one out of the wet bars re-frid-a-rator; sat back on the couch, for a little re-coop session, flipped on the re-mote con-trol T.V. and without the real ability to enjoy myself in that situation flipped the channels until I found something in English and sat it out for a time.

The jet lag it wasn't bad, it never really is going in the direction of the West, the West to reach the ever so alluring East. Mostly it is just like staying up later, later than the my normal standards, the way late that I stay up in and until in L.A. Going East to reach the West, the first world, Europe now that throws me off, day to night, night to day, wake up 3:00 AM with nada to do; that's all a different story though, a different time frame all together.

The visual presentations were boring; I pulled the curtains in the various directions of view throughout the city, looked but saw nada. You know it is a little bit hard to explain and many would probably doubt the validity of the statement but there comes a point out there on the hard road when you have just seen it all.

Places, they may be different, pictures on the mind's eye. People, culture, call it what you will, but some how it all just seems so fucking much the same. It is not that it is boring but it is just that once you see the pit of society one too many times, it no longer holds much allure, thought in truth it obviously still does tend to call me out. And I mean come on, I am just not one of those dudes who likes to go chill his session on some beach catching some rays, or in some bullshit tourist type attractions.

So lost, alone, nowhere really to go, yet everywhere to be. Yes, life it is a paradox.

I had noticed one of the cameras which I had pulled along for the ride, was beginning to have some problems, its shutter was not releasing properly, so I took a few to play with its inner workings but without the proper tools little could be done, fuck it, I threw it on the couch, one of the couches.

I looked at the T.V., I viewed the view, I gazed around the room, contemplating my folly, thinking this is how I should be living but than all the anxiety of my financial woos came to mind, I felt fucked, Presidential Suite and all.

*   *   *

cross a bridge
any bridge
dreams are the cause
promised on the other side
cross a bridge
any bridge
live any dream
that is haveable
take it to the limit
they say there lies the answer
there the answer it will be found
take it to the limit
but they lied
I know this to be true
I have been there
and found only further nothing
and if the dreams
if they all could come true
would this world not be a far better place
but cross the bridge
what do you find
life wrapped up
truth wrapped up
answers wrapped up
in a sealed envelope
hidden form the view
hidden from the eyes

the answer placed neatly inside
so there is nothing
nothing that can be seen
cross a bridge
any bridge
there the answers are promised
to be found
cross a bridge
any bridge
there the dreams are held
hand them to me
hand them
to
me
for the hidden truth
have remained wrapped far to long
I have looked
and I have seen
nothing

*   *   *

Hunger, it was pushing the lunch time hour. As I had bailed the hotel in the AM nada was happening as of yet in the chow lines so I passed it off and over, now it was time to eat.

Down, I go, down the elevator I go, past the strategically placed floor man at the pulpit, down in the realms of the not so abundant, in terms   of   the finances. I passed the desk, the main desk, the reservation desk, the check-in desk, I thought to ask if they had a room for me yet, a movement I knew was impending, unable to forget about. No, I'll check it after a little meal session.

I walked past the area of the Philippine night folk, where lousy renditions of 1970's pop had been sung last night, the night before; uck, it was bad but the Philippine people for some reason dig that shit. Down the stairs a bit farther, lunch time...

They were wrapping up the breakfast buffet as I pulled in and the a-number-one lunch buffet would not be put out for twenty or thirty, "Did I want to come back," I was asked, "No, I'll just pull on in here for a bit and see what the menu has to offer."

It sucked, the sandwich was greasy, and the java was bad. The high point of the lunch was when this bad little mouse came chilling by, hiding   from the encroaching realms of civilization. From this table, to the counter. From the counter to behind exposed and chrome, desert refrigerator. All to the amusement of me, all to the complaints of the, 'way too important and cool, to good for all that,' tourist that inhabited the rest of the dinning facility. "If you don't dig it, go back to the West," I thought. Though the bad attitude hostess, a bus boy or three tried to get the bad little bastard, he escaped their pursuit. Finally, through with the food, it made me sick, through with the no more cup fulls of java, I bailed on.

The desk, "No, Mr. Shanti, we do not have a room for you as of yet, you will have to spend another night in the Presidential Suite. Were sorry."

Oh fuck, I was going to have to spend another night in the Presidential Suite, is there no justice in this world?

But with that, I was out on the street again. I, of course, had to go put the main hello to the floor dude again en route, out-route to get my cameras, even pulled the one along which had not been a-working oh too well. Down the elevator, back out on the streets; the streets that is where I belong.

I paced it out to the main drag; a half a block over or so, to the right, over that way, it call me down and out. When I'm travelin', when I'm walkin' I just always follow my feelings.

The sun it was pacing me now, from the pale of the AM morning to the early PM shine, it was hot, way hot, crystal blue-sky, white-hot sun. I wondered did it see me, did it know I was there.

I cruised on, past the local Golden Arches, they were everywhere now. I remember the Asian time when that wasn't the case.

Up ahead there seemed to be lying in my foot path over to the further right a bit of a local shopping mall. The initial rush of the heat had hit me a bit hard after my chill down session at lunch so I thought I would go and give it a view.

The main gates, the main doors, they were to my right, right again a bad little uniformed dude, searching all those that were about to go it. I mean this was becoming an anarchical society and all with the just jumping the wire of the Marcos' era a short time before. Over to my left was this guy sitting at a folded out table selling Bali Song, Butterfly Knives for sale. Yes, I had already had my experience with those bad little pups upon my arrival to the Philippines.

Last night, the night before, into town a bit late and in my general, well... let's get what we can kind and type of mood decided to put my steak out on the streets and see what was a-have-able. So post the check-in to the now legendary Presidential Suite, I put my rocket in my pocket and my butt in gear and was in movement to the outer realms of truth, love, lust, and civilization.

Down the elevator, I proceeded, hotel lobby, it was dark, brown toned and stiff. I, heard   some music, followed the sound, it was the previous aforementioned rendition rock of pop top-forty U.S. style. There was a couple or two dancing, Philippine style, a drunk or three, even a lady or three, out and about looking available so I plopped myself down to see what action my be held in the works.

I sat and listen to the music—music that no self respecting music aficionado like myself would be caught dead listing too. It was like straight off the Sonny and Cher or Tony Orland and Dawn T.V. shows of the early 1970's, mega uck.

I sat back and awaited a waitress to put her form in my direction; drink in mind. I sat back and awaited a sweet, fine and priceable piece of ass to plant herself, give me a glance, give me a stare, my direction please, but nothing, nada. I mean now call me an impatient person but post about ten minutes of sitting there without even a greyhound, my typical and preferred travel drink, to sooth the sounds of that shit music which was vibrating in my ears, I was out-a-there.

I moved down the brown stairs, the door, the door where the airport taxi driver had let me out was in sight, but there behind me flashed a light, several light, flashing, flashing bulbs. Blinking to so sort of Philippine rhythm, red and blue and green and yellow. It was the hotel discothèque, well I have had more than one party scene present itself to me in Asian locations such as this, so in I turn, in I go. I pay the entrance fee to some sweet semi fine golden skinned lady of the perpetual night, oh yes, I love them, ladies of the perpetual night.

Inside, dead... A Philippine couple or two, or three dancing to the UK English sounds, a drunk or three partied down swaying to the beat, nothing worth initially grabbing onto but than you never know, so down I planted myself, chilled down a greyhound or three, well maybe four. The barkeep left my dead soldier(s) in front of me, I guess to remind a person of what a drunk, they were or were not.

Awaiting a reason not to be alone, none came into sight or vision. The music I had heard before, in every pumping disco from Taipei to Bombay. The elixir, well I had tasted before, most would say one too many times. Nothing to hold me, no reason to stay, outside, that is where the dreams always are, outside... I was gone.

Out the large glass door of the hotel par excellence I proceed. Glass so fragile. One thing on my mind, well, no need to say, I am sure that you know what it is.

"Where are you going," comes a voice form the realms of the semi intoxicated night.
"Just walking."
"You want a woman?"
"No, just walking."

The voice of an all night taxicab driver, there were several lined up in wait. Asia, the night, they are always there, the taxicab drivers, that wish to take you to the oh so alluring momentary nothingness in the meaningless arms of a singular and oh so poetic whore.

I turn them, the drivers down, as I generally chose to do. Me, I prefer the chase. Me, I prefer the chance, the dance of the chance. The reason that if it comes, I will cum. With every dance there is another chance...

"You should not go walking in that direction."

Left, I had turned left and was proceeding left along the hotel wall into the darken reaches of the night.

"Why?"
"It is not safe there."

I just looked at him and smiled, me being the bad dude that I think that I am walked on.

Yes, this was the back side, the back side and the underside of this stretch of Manila property. I saw it the moment I left the hotel lights.

A parking lot, large and empty, to my right, the wall, the hotel to my left. I moved on. I reached a right angle, a turn, darkness up ahead. A street, a block in that direction, seemed a logical location as only shadows live in the night.

As I walked, I head voice(s), Tagalog, the Philippine tongue, being spoken up ahead. In a stairwell, dark as the beings which inhabit the night, three were sitting there, drunk as it sounded, they could not help be notice my white form.

Move on, I thought with a feeling of intensity, urgency, adrenal rush. Move on I did. Fifteen, twenty, maybe a hundred yards as I moved towards the light from the night, I don't know, movement lost its actual binding realms.

I heard it coming from my side, not coming from behind, the flip, the swish, the slight clanging of metal to metal of a Bali Song, Butterfly Knife, opening. Yes, I was familiar with the sound, for I possessed a version of two of my own back in L.A. Yes, I knew what was coming, my heart it began to pound. I walked close to the wall, kept the angle of attack coming from only one direction. I made my self breath deep, slow, down the heart beating, clarity is what I needed, not false anticipation.

I thought to run, run for the light, the light of the distant street which now seemed miles away. I did not know the terrain, I did not know what to expect, I knew if I ran, and if they ran faster it would only mean an exhausted Bali Song in the back, I would prefer to look it in the eyes.

Movement came, it was swift: one, two, it was two. They came up through their shadows blending in the night. One had a white shirt on, just for the record, thin what I thought to be blue stripes. They other shirt red, red like the color of oxidized blood, blood and a knife, a very fair combination.

A word was spoken, a word I could not understand, I felt their closeness to me, closer, closer, more of a feeling than a sight. The knife, one, yes two, there was a vague reflection in the pale dark blue moon light.

Closer, closer more words were spoken, their knifes low and ready to strike. In range, in focus, no time to talk, threaten or play games, the first one, white shirt gave me target, front kick full on, full power right into the base of his chin. He flew back, no time to delay; red, to the right, my right, his left; down, as my leg came down, feel it, I can not see it, a thousand moments lived in the one millisecond of time, my inner voice spoke, down, down side kick, right across his knee. I heard the bones snap, I heard him scream.

Now it was time to run. Back, back to the hotel, safety, such as safety was. I saw the stairwell patrons step from behind their veil, I thought, would they stop me, no I ran out, splash, I was in some mud, I ran around them as they yelled something at me, turn the corner back the other way, light was more present, I could see the taxi coming up. I was at the door, I slowed down.

"What's the matter? I told you it was dangerous."
"Fuck you!" I said.

I walked in, up the stairs, up to the elevator, I began, as I always do, post a confrontation, to shake from all the adrenalin. I shook as the elevator went up. 10, 11, 12, the floors went by. I breathed deep, tried to control it, 19, 20, 21, penthouse. I got there, walked into the hall, fucked around in the dark until I could find the fucking light switch and the wet bar, mini bar, doused down a brew from Holland, laid back, breathed deep.

"Fuck you," I thought.

*   *   *

I checked out the bad little knives over to the far side of midnight on the right, my left of the security guard who was checking all those who entered the shopping mall. My first thought was to buy one or two, I flipped them open and closed, checked their construction, ecteetera-a-mundo. Then the realization came that it would not be that wise of a purchase, at least at this point due to the military security dude checking the credentials of all who enter. Yes, he was Philippine military.

So I chilled back, I walked past, headed for the door of the cool down mall. You see, in addition to not wanting to add insult to injury with the purchasing of a local Butterfly Knife, I had in my pocket, stashed down deep in my way baggy pants, the black Swiss Army Knife that I always pack in my travels. Not as fast, in the opening departmento as say a Bali Song but then never a problem a customs either.

79

My heart kicked up a few beats per minute as I approached the door, the line, though it was short, to the door; expecting to be searched, just as the others, integrated just the same.

Me, I walked up and soul boy enlisted man just waved me on through. AOK in my department. I guess he figured I was not going to one of the people that have any reason to blow up the mall. Funny, I probably have more reasons.

*   *   *

You know it was all like the L.A. Watts Riots back in '66. I lived there then. Yeah, I know, white boy and living there, (then), that's a long story though. But to the point, it was like there they were all the local indigenous population running around blowing up their own bros property, their own bros businesses, their own bros Cadillacs.

The National Guard were brought in, I remember them driving in troop carriers, jeeps, tanks all up and down the street that I lived on. Believe me, it was a scary experience for a little white boy honky like myself.

The point I am trying to make here though is, I mean I never understood why did they go and trash their own zone of cribs.   I mean if they wanted to make a statement they should have cruised on up to Beverly Hills and trashed the placed, like the old saying, I remember hearing once, you don't shit in your own back yard.

So why would the Philippine locals do so much trashing of their own turf. Sure, I know, the rich, the affluent, and all that, but still this is all their home .

But give anyone a ticket to power and the fool will always take it by the balls.

Inside the mall, I strolled around, checking out the this and that, a book that I would come back later for, didn't want to carry it around. Fashion Passion down to the minimal in this fashionless mall, I mean it wasn't Melrose or the Beverly Center back in L.A., or Harajuku in Tokyo after all.

MostI was checking out, the babes that were checking me out, 'oh yes, it did all seem like it was going to be easy prey,' I wanted to scream, in all my tones of approval.

Nothing really held me there, back out on the street. Movement to no movement, movement in the heat. To my right, the original direction intended, I moved proceeding along.

*　　*　　*

the heat
it closes in
like the nowhere
like the nothing
the nothing that takes
its whole possession of the soul
and the day
shows the light
light
where the shadows of the sun
may be found
many run from here
me, I ran to here
I look around myself
and I wonder why
where there is no shadows
there is no light
and this light
prey down on me
with full on intensity
the light
the heat
the need for movement

the need to move out
the need to find
find, what I am looking for
what am I looking for
here in this light
here in this heat
there is no where to run
it is deadly in its destiny
it calls me out
like the pagan scream of a vampire
in the depths of the night
calling to all of its dark servants
blood upon its mind
as they hate the night
I hate the day
but called out to it
just and still the same
nowhere to run
no way to get there
still I must go
I must try to find
what was never there to begin with
light without shadow
night without day

*   *   *

This bad little dude walks up to me, as I stroll in the shear density of the surfaced heat, my body is covered with sweat; inside outside, the face, the arms, the legs inside the clothing, my dick, my balls. I would have prefer a babe of one sort, free or otherwise or another to come up to me, speak of let's go have a soda, lets be friends, tell me that they don't like Ronald Regan, I can/could confer to that as neither do I.

It was out in front of this soda shop, an in the air soda shop on the street and I should have seen it coming; me in all my traveled-ness, my journeyman level into the Asian days and nights, but no I got sucked in, suckered in as only a believer can do. So yeah, I sat down with the guy, maybe fortyish, and listened as he told me of his prison woes.

You see, this all was, it took place at a time, the Marcos booted out of time, space, money, and power; their power, the people pain, it had happened the month before I believe, a month maybe two. They were out, the political tortured prisoners, who protested for their freedom, demonstrated for a chance, well they were tossed behind the bars, and I had seen pictures of what those bars were like back home in the U.S., 'Sixty Minutes' and all. So, I had a certain compassion for the what this old dude must have been through, I guess that is what got me to sit down, sit down and talk for awhile.

He had done his time. Time in the amount of four years as I had been told. Done his time, adding up to nothing; as we are all doing our time sitting back here on earth. For some though it must be far more painful but any good mystic will tell you that it is all a state of mind, as any good yogi would tell you that this body it is a prison and we all really want to be free. Well be that as it is, be that as it may, I would far prefer to be in this body and out, than that body and in, doing time for no good reason than for politics and power and people putting money in Swiss bank accounts.

He had done his time, now was out, three days, he said, "Lets sit down, drink from the same bottle," in separate glasses of course, "Let us be friends."

He poured the Pepsi, over dirty ice that I worried about, we drank, sat back, talked of his fate, of my fate, "An artist," so I answered; dreams and sin, my resume by any other name.

"Can you give me some money? I want to return to my family in Cebu City. They have not seen me for so long a time. Can you give me some money, the boat leaves, in three hours, a boat that I, I must be on."

I gave him some money. So much for our friendship, so much for our Pepsi. To jump ahead of myself and the storyline; no, I never saw him again. A con maybe; a Pilipino, no doubt; return to Cebu City, well who really knows, left to literature in the pagan white man's hand.

I moved on...

The ocean lay a block or so over to my left, the divine mother and all of her assets. I knew this from my view of the surroundings, my view from my hotel Presidential Suite.

The ocean she always calls me, the ocean, here or in Asia, always seems to speak my name, walk down to here, walk next to here; left, I moved to the left.

*　　*　　*

and if there is no other reason
if there is no longer any dream in sight
when I have no more reason to pretend
and my tears continue to fill my lonely night
then it is to you
that I go to
to you
that I turn
the sound that roars its cosmic message
without thought or mind
it is to you that I am called
to merge and live
within your omnipresence
a spell that has been cast by god
to give new birth
to all things
and when it is time
for this body to end
when my life has been pulled
from my hands
it will be to you that I go
like a rain drop

entering the holy sea
one merging with the whole
and living on forever and ever

*   *   *

I walked past this little restaurant called, Aristocrat, nothing much to mention, except in its tourist call-ness but a thought to the mind, that so many of these American influenced populous thinks/thought that the pearly gates of the U.S. dollars: the fame, the fortune, the streets paved with gold were strategically lying just ahead, over the Green Card hill.

I guess I can't blame people for anything, any dream must have been better that/this.

The water, the ocean water, it was polluted: dirty, green, and brown. There were war ships in the harbor, flying the U.S. and various other flags, mostly there were tankers, tankers and cargo ships, dumping and polluting taking what they can, leaving the remains for the rest. Sheading waste, while young boys and girls nakedly swam in the waters below.

I walked upon this levy ledge; young, seeking that feeling of freedom, lost but than never really known, just the dance in the chance. The city next to me, only the heart beat of a small park, and a main street away, the ocean next to me; left on the black hand side.

I walked on the cement ledge, took a photo or three. Took one of this little beggar family, tried to bail gratis, but ended up throwing some change their way. I mean it was only fair, the price of a photo and all.

That was my mistake thought for a shit-load of kids attached themselves to me, money they wanted, money that they were not going to get, I mean it is not that I am not a generous person and sure I toss some change in the direction of the poor quite often, following my feelings and all, but some how it never really changes anything, somehow it never really seems to help, somehow there are times when I just don't feel like getting hustled anymore, I mean what are they doing saving up for college?

The park, maybe a hundred feet across, it was dirty, the water was dirty, the kids were dirty, they kept grabbing at me, trying to stick their hand(s) in my pockets, I had to chill them off, I then had to head trip about getting lice or some disease from them.

The sky though, I looked up through the trees, and being over to the side of the rising building of the material world, the sky, it was blue, blue crystal and there and than, it is not the heat, not the dirt, not the kids, or the money, that I remember, but the crystal blue color of the sky, (is crystal, the color blue? I think not).

Up a little farther on, as this walk continued, a young, well dress guy, said to be a college boy, a college boy and with no money to pay for tuition pulled himself up next to me, next to me and chasing the remaining children off. The typical questions, wanted to know where I was from, no not Germany, if I could help him out, in the dollar department. It was Ok if I gave him U.S. currency, so he said. No doubt. But I gave him zero and walked on. If he was a she it all may have been a different story as then the she and the I may have had a deal to make but the he and the he's just not interested in the lie. A woman, she can lie to me anytime. Lie to me.

Physical

I went, I had a physical today. A physical if you know what I mean. The doctor she was this short, dark, plump, little bombshell. She did have a look about her. One of those tea kettles that were screaming and about to explode.

She sat me down on the table of examination. I was clad in no clothes, the nurse, she had asked me to remove them just minutes before. She gave me a paper nightgown to place upon my form. She was out, I was in, in it that is, I was alone, it the cold pale off white of an examination room.

The Doc, she came in, looking like a placid polyester pavement princess who had had too much to eat. "How are you today," she said as she yawned. "Too much action huh," I thought in my mind, but I just said, "fine."

"Breath in, breath out," she told me as she pulled down my gown on the right sleeve side of the night. It was obvious that she wanted it; I could feel that cold touch of pressure, that touch I had felt so many times before.

"Lay down," she said, lay down I did. She pulled up my paper napkin gown exposing all of my pride. She touched, she pushed, she massaged, "I have paid women to do these same things to me," "Cough," she said.

Pudgy

I made ready for the day, out. As I did the thought, as I looked at myself in the mirror, came to me, my hair looking good, the clothing which I had chosen green, mystical green, I looked like me. I walked into the living room and picked up my new, new in relation to my others, camera. Taking the already in place film from its chambers I replaced it with print film, unlike the slide film I generally use which had occupied it previously. Loading the new film and grabbing my mini tripod, my main and or other one(s) currently being in my storage unit, I went out to my ocean front patio and took a few self-timered photos of myself with the intention of sending them to my sweet little, ever-faithful, awaiting Chinese princes in the Peoples Republic, which I like to call the P.R.

She quite unlike my current, local, and aforementioned (M.S.L.C.A.V.T.P.) is quite Asian in nature. Not the syndrome of what as happen to the C.A. (California Asian) girls trying to foolish adapt and be accepted, becoming quite a slut in the process. Anyway aside for my camera falling off my table on the patio and hitting the cement quite un-ballet like, I took the photos standing there in true self timer egotism style complete with an occasional frame of a wave and so on. The only problem was when I rewound the film, automatic(ly) as this camera is designed it did not realize it was half the roll and would not completely rewind. So and thus I ended up having to trash the roll and only having slide film in my box of film did not take any further photographs. Was god telling me something? Giving me a sign?

The weather was holding true as I headed out to my wintertime convertible car, top already down. It was warm, warm for winter, maybe seventy-five degrees or so on the Fahrenheit scale. The sun was out. I thought how this would be a good opportunity to get the sun tan line on my forehead removed. The one I had picked up in Japan last summer, with my hair parted on the side. Now it is combed straight back and though it has been so for several months, I have not been out in the daytime weather enough, being onto sleep in and all, enough to get it remove. It is not all that noticeable. One of those things that I probably notice but no one else.

My first destination on my way out and into and on to the city was to pick up a wee little bit of breakfast. Now, it is not that I was all that hungry. Having had a mucho supply of the Mexican food last night, combined with the margaritas of course. But in any situation where there is a calling out, a going out, there needs to be a diversion in mind. The first one on my agenda was this sweet little thirty plus specimen who seemed and appeared to be giving me more than the eye the last few times I was in there.

It's funny as one ages, not that I'm old, but pushing thirty fast, it is interesting how my tastes have changed. How the older women thirty plus seem to hold so much more in promised illusion.

The sun was warm and I headed in the direction of my mystical and special dreamer breakfast alone. I invited her, (M.S.L.C.A.V.T.P.) but I guess dreamers tend to eat alone.

I park; I push back my long hair having been thoroughly and thankfully fully blown in the wind. There was a couple exiting their car at the same time as I was. A couple of the mindless and should be mid-western, instead they just perpetuated their lower middle class-ness in the apparel which they wore. I walked, they walked, one of those times of who gets to the door first. I did, I held it for them.

There she was the waitress of desire, such as waitress desire is. I mean I am zero into waitresses, yet this one had a look and for someone like myself, an out-there mystical, lusty dreamer, her look did promise illusion. I mean hey, I did go back to check it out again.

She is white, wonder white bread to the max. I keep promising myself no more white bread but in a world where I seem to eat all my meals a restaurants I somehow am presented with the menu as such. Sometimes you eat something just to try it out, yes?

She sat me down in all her white breadedness, smiles on her face. Her typically American restaurant uniform spoke of the slight amounts of pudg which obviously lay beneath. Yet I had noticed that before and yet I still held an interest. White bread and pudgy to match, what is going wrong with me?

Relationships

A year long, a year later, one of those bullshit relationships, that go nowhere so fast that it makes the wind swirl through your hair and the gods stop and take notice. You know the type, everything adds to nothing and all that is gained is wasted time and not being alone. For oh yes, the reason of predominance that most of us hold on to the non-solitary, the not being alone. The hermits are the saints, the loners. The fools are those like me that live the lie and stay when walking would have been so much better.

I guess I should have read the sighs painted upon the wall, seen the pictures in their frames, "Blue sheets, why do guy always have blue sheet?" First words out of her mouth as she came over to crib down crib central for the first time around. Love session in progress, I mean hey, I don't want to hear statements of what she has seen before.

I don't know, you know how it goes, some chicks, well most chicks, they just love to rap, to lie, to tell the mostly fraudulent stories of their past. I guess they think it impresses dudes, believe me it does not. This chick, the chick in question, one year later and all, man she was one on the serious side of the lets talk shit, bullshit, you know more like a dude than a chick. In regards to the sense of how dude sit around and rap all kinds of pagan garbage that is little or no based in fact.

After telling me she was power plowed by six dudes, one day,

"Didn't you feel used?"
"Maybe, I was using them."

Maybe so, I don't know, but this is a pretty sad world, if a chick as pretty as her has to get the power pile driver done (in) by six dudes to feel AOK. A slut, yeah I thought that she was, but I guess that is just a definition in a world that in all truth lacks any. Push comes, to shove, six months down the road, as my buddy Saturday Jim said it would come to pass, yeah that too was a let's rap the bullshit lie.

93

So anyway, should have walked then, but the thing is where do you walk too? Yeah, I did my usual take off for Asia, once or twice on her, but money it is tight this time in my life and debt well... I would have gone a lot more but... So I have hung out, made the mistake of spending too much go nowhere money on her and/or us and I let the year slip on by.

The two biggest mistakes of life, spending danero on unworthy causes, and letting time slip on by. But than we could speak philosophy, money spent on not being alone, like buying the time of a whore, and time, what does it mean anyway?

Her past, though, always hung over our relationship's head, she brought it, I did not ask for it. Insecure, not really, I just think that the world should and/or could revolve around me. Mostly...

Siam Tracy

to Hae Won:
the woman who all others
should be judge by

I remember the days on the Mekong. The heat that pounded onto my soul as I stare into the distance and knew that that there was no place left to run. So I stayed, I stared into the emptiness and watched as the waters of the river poured down, carrying all of existences: life, death, passion, and agony. Its brownness whispered the name of it origin high in the Himalayas, atop the plains of the Tibetan Plateau.

Sometimes the clouds would etch the sky with visions of wonder as I would look deeply into the wisdom of their whiteness. Yes, it is then that I would know of their origin. Yes, the knowledge from the plains of Tibet above me, where a million generations of yogis had sought their enlightenment in the dark distant and hidden realms of the absolute.

Was their wisdom flowing down to me here there as I stared onto the river, to the scene of Laos across the river from me? Or perhaps the clouds were my witness to illumination as I sat in my hut of a home, supported by stilts and watched life's journey pass in front of me.

I witnessed it: life; the Mekong and wondered how could destiny have led me here; on this journey of enlightenment; day in, day out, in the pouring, the pounding heat of Siam. But there in the distance in the memory, the cool, the snow, the raging enlightenment of Mila Repa and the promise of illuminating conquest in Tibet. But that was another time, another journey, another story. This was life, this was Thailand, and all that matters is the now…

*   *   *

Another day awoke to its own vision and I rose from my bed. It was this rather cool little apparatus, the bed that is actually more or less Western style. I stared up into the aloneness of the mosquito net that enveloped me. Yeah, there was a dead one or thirty of them attached to the bad lad. But, all life is death, yes?

The morning awoke way hot as they all tended to do. The heat pounces on your soul there on the deep side of Southeast Asia. Somehow, however, there was a reason a purpose in all of the sweat. A reason felt, but impossible to explain.

How can one explain the foundation of purpose and the enlightenment found in the realms of humanity so distant, so lost in its own abyss? This had become my home.

We all have a reason to hide, if we look for one. Yeah it is the same old story: some from the law, some from love, some for love, some like myself, for no better reason that the belief in the dream and the path of and/or to enlightenment had led me on a different road then that of the average.

But poetry based philosophy aside, I mean like, fuck it all, what could it all mean, and on to the story.

Tracy Delany is the name, just a name like all others, so temporary. I had bagged it on into Thailand in my mid verging on my late twenties. Yeah, late by some standards but I had been living on the far side of midnight over India way, so early or late was just a point of view.

I had returned there too, come back like here to Thailand. I was looking, seeking, searching for something. It wasn't like when I had first gone there, Mother India, when I was young; no. I had realized all of the hypocrisy of the life of a holy man long ago. You know, like all of the reinforcement is there.

They tell you, they promise you the forever in enlightenment, in eternity; what does that all mean anyway? I mean like, you fully feel all so holy, and you are told that it is so. The people they touch your feet. You feel so fucking superior, just because you wear the orange robes and the prayer beads.

The yogi's reassure you that the nothing is the everything. And as fully true as that all may be; I mean like man, let's get way real.

I guess in retrospect, I don't even really know why I returned, for I had given up the orange robes and the title lifetimes ago. Maybe salvation, yes salvation: from the streets, from pumping too hard against the nighttime abyss. Yeah, I had this babe once, she told me that it was so. She told me that is why I seek the truth. Yeah, and I heard it once spoken that the mark of a truly functioning person in a full on functioning society is small talk. I fucking hate small talk.

Anyway, I'm deviating again, going into life philosophy. But anyway that is what led me here. I was no stranger to the out-back.

*　　　*　　　*

The days sometimes, I would be awoken early. The boats, these local long boats; yeah, they were way long and way thin; motored by an engine mounted on the back.

In the heat it is hard to sleep very late anyway. Not like the days in L.A. when the dream would pound so hard into the night, that the morning would never wake until the afternoon was fully coming on.

But I was awoken. I stared beyond the net that held me bound. Like bars into a night leading to a day that screamed to be released. The mosquitos, the sounds of the boats going somewhere to nowhere out there on the river, my eyes open; death, it was all around.

and the wisdom it cries out to us
wailing to whip away the lies
and life, it pushes on to nowhere
where life ultimately exists

97

Have you ever felt it, the heat that bangs down on the soul. Yeah, I am sure that you have. Uncomfortable passion(s), it is hard to breath as its essence comes down.

Passion, a name I know all too well. I glanced to the right of me; nude, there she laid; a golden body which had embraced my being. I could the sweat which had gathered upon her nude skin. Her straight, jet-black hair iced the silence of the now fading semi clean white sheet which we had laid upon. Passion, yes, I will just call her Passion.

I rose from my landing, another day, another dream to be had. Well, at least the alive to be living. Have you ever noticed stuck in the alive? Alive is all that we know. It is
all that we will ever know. Many claim to know more, I don't believe them.

As I rose the pagan blue of the sky crossed my vision as I passed the open window.

Open window, what a joke. The windows were either open or open.

Someday Girl

It was Santa Cruz in the early seventies. Spirituality was in the air. I was young, seventeen. No desires but no desire at all, no goals but enlightenment. Times they were free.

I was clad, as were many, in white yogi draw string pants, sandals, and a mala, (Indian prayer beads,) around my neck.

Shaving, never did it. My beard, such as it was, like my hair, was long.

They say Eastern Spirituality took hold of America in the sixties but I disagree. Its root may have taken hold then but it did not bloom until the seventies. Now in the late eighties it has quite unfortunately withered and become overrun by the weeds known as yuppies, chasing materialistic ideals and BMWs. It is a different age indeed.

May I make a deviation from the centerline here and tell a brief interlude of a minor story. Two weeks previous a friend of mine, a female friend, a yuppie friend, she told me the story, made the statement, "The Yuppies are dead." I had to inquire, "Did they have a funeral?" I remember the death of the hippies, a word provocated by the press. Yuppies perhaps are provocated by the same. Did they die the same? Somehow their meaning seems so much more meaningless.

Anyway, it was the seventies, that was before the inception of the red neck hippies that now inhabit the streets of Santa Cruz taking the place of the truth seekers of the time. The only definition of a person was the length of their hair. The name of the game was parted down the middle. The only order of business was chanting East Indian spiritual hymns with American accents.

I was young but had already done my time on the hard road. Heading up to San Francisco and Canada for years before. But than came the involvement spirituality in its maiden form. No longer was it, I and my buddy named Vince, trudging seeking alone. I had been initiated he had gone to college and given up the dream and was smoking dope.

The Heat

The temperature had risen. Hot, it had become hot. I never feel good, I never feel comfortable in The Heat.

*　　　*　　　*

The Heat
it falls like rain
its impact is far more devastating
far more deadly
moving in deep
taking no prisoners
pulling out the soul
with the jagged teeth
of the serpent

The Heat
it is not for the
faint of heart

*　　　*　　　*

The scene, like other scenes, different, yet not different, a sight to the field of vision. A photograph to the mind's eye. A swamp flanked by a river. A river bounded by a swamp. Dark and muddy river: green, yellow, and brown swamp. The water merged into the land, the water joined with the sky, fusing itself into The Heat, humidity was its child.

I was living next to them; the river and the swamp. I was living within them the humidity and The Heat.

No way in, no way out.

Laying in bed, dreams they were completed, the waking space, the distance, still had its hold on my soul. Clouded vision, a hope for another scene: trees, blue sky, clear river, pleasant mountain dirt roads, clean, somewhere clean, not so lost to the incoming destruction of time, of man.

Moving; finally from the clean white sheets, passing across the room looking outside. No, no mountains; no, no streams, the scene was only in my mind; for this was Southeast Asia.

*   *   *

in The Heat
the things they seem distant
in The Heat
the things
they seem far away
the moisture moving through the air
makes life
all so surreal
I look
I see
but I never really see

*   *   *

It was in the late night, in an all night restaurant, 24 hrs a day. She sat across from me at the dining table, I stared at her, she appeared so different than the woman who I had known just an hour or two before.

Her face, it had been dried by her tears, her skin showed the signs of white flakey fragments in place but ready to fall. Her eyes they were Asian swollen, red, and lost. In all of this passion she appeared almost innocent, almost renewed, yet, I knew our love would never be the same. The magic had been crushed.

and when the truth comes out
it does break hard
truth that should have been know all along

*   *   *

Mornings are always hard for me, even if, as they generally do, my mornings beginning in the early afternoon. The morning, The Heat...

I stood there staring in to the abyss of the swamp, of the river for a moment or three; the telephone rang. It was a babe, a babe from a long time ago, a long time ago babe, who I had walked face to face into two days previously, two days after my return.

Yes, I had returned, re-entered, came back from my so called home; America, L.A. Yes, I had reappeared into the world where I may gaze upon the river, upon the swamp each morning, each day, each evening. Came back to where the world, where I was lost deeply in the night.

Yes, I do have that karmic habit, that unplanned destiny of meeting/re-meeting those of my past, those who I would feel, I would think, I would prefer that I would never see again.

It was on the street, a street where the street vendors dwell, selling their fake European watches, selling their counterfeit leather bags, to counterfeit people, commonly known as tourists. I was walking, she was looking, she turned, we met, eye to eye.

From there the transfigurations and their applications hold little importance, we yelled, we screamed, we cried, we made love. It was her, on the telephone again, the day later, the next day, this day.

"Do you want to be with me?"

The question seems eternally posed to me. Women, they seem to need some sort of continued assurance that men are not simply basking in their physical form. As it be truly known, however, females are generally the one relishing in the male form of support, carnal knowledge, and impossible life security. Doing this, while holding the collar leash of guilt, telling their partner that they, are not doing, are not providing, sufficient amount(s) of love, money, social activities, etcetera-a-mundo.

The night, the nights of Southeast Asia seemed a better alternative to me, I told her so.

*   *   *

Looking around the restaurant, the place old, the people old, the food old; I ate mine, she played with hers. The atmosphere brown and depressing. The outside night time sky wailed.

"You have never given us a chance."

Chances, who do you give them to, how are they worded, what form do they take? Is not simply placing oneself in the presence of another chance enough? Then the form may be looked at, the pattern developed.

No, there she was again, blaming me? Placing condemnation upon me, when in truth, as I viewed/review the occurrence, no longer could I hold any of the fault.

I told her so.

The waitress, old, a little fat, placed the bill upon our table. I looked around myself, checked for a glimpse, a hold on reality. The feeling/that feeling, the night seemed vague, abstract.

*   *   *

blow a wind
blow it into my night
my night of truth
my night of sin
like all the previous nights
my night of The Heat
The Heat
when The Heat got too hot
the night
when it was too dark
dark
brown
and old
let the wind breath
breath its cooling breath
as the truth is known

as the truth is told
let it cool me down

*   *   *

The telephone marathon session began, like so many before, so many to come; words lost to no ones ears, for no one, neither one of us was listening.

"Would you like me to come over?"

"Why," reverberates in my mind, than the thought of lust, love, pulsating artistic passion comes to mind; I give the go ahead.

Moving across the room, back to the semi clean white sheets; pull them over my head. "Why," again comes to mind. Why did I say AOK, why did I not choose no, why's and wherefores, there is so many other things which I should do.

It the realm of the semi clean, semi white, the semi darkening white, enclosed, exposed to only my own thought, my own reality, my world, the only one that matters, I, I fall back into the arms of sleep.

*   *   *

the remembrances of the night
calling back
calling me back
where the realms of safety
exist
where the realms of reality
are so hard
not so short lived
somewhere
where it is easier
somewhere

*   *   *

In the realms of passive awareness where the moments are so real; so real, more real, than of those which reality chooses to hold and call its own. Reality, its names and forms, they never seemed all too defined to my minds eye. It all seems too temporal, to affected by momentary thoughts, momentary passions, emotions, etcetera...

The pictured, the script, playing upon my inner eyelid cinema; crowed it was crowded, not jammed like the afternoon road ways of Bangkok, or the six o'clock subways of Tokyo but proper like the evening train stations of Zurich, of London, yes it was a train station in the U.K.

I was there, there the gray immensity of the pillars and the rounded ceiling raised miles above my head. I remember a vague image of a lady, a Caucasian, brown haired, light brown, to my left but my mind was more involved with the masses around me and my direction to my destination: a train, the train.

But there, in all that structural enormity, in all that populace immensity just as I began to move, in my back, my lower left back, it came, a knife, a stab, I had been mortally wounded.

In that second, I jumped from my sleep, and viewed the woman who had touched, who was touching me in the exact same, apparent real life, spot. The apparent spot of my destruction. It was her, my semi-invited guest. Tall, dark, and Asian.

Long ago as a child, a blossoming adult, grown up too soon, I had come to realize that dreams, the false reality as they may be known, were lived, could be lived in only seconds. Hours, days, weeks, years, may pass in the blink of the eye, in and to the/this non-material world.

This knowledge came to me as I slept in our small semi funky inner city Los Angeles apartment, upon a blue coach. Dozing off, I lived a dream, a long encounter only to be woken by a passing truck noise and glancing across the room to the clock and calculating my actual nap time as having been less than two minutes, I realized all could be lived in such a short amount of physical time.

naps, such a FA, (fine art)
few ever develop the technique or ability
as my living years have continued
and days
and time
seem to weather much too fast
I take refuge
in knowing of this other world
where time is not so foolishly bound
by a/the clock
tick tock
fuck the clock

*   *   *

I stared up, looking into the space which lay within her eyes. I felt a dissatisfaction come over me, a certain disgust with allowing myself once again to be caught by her entrapment.

Addiction, it is only for the few.
Compulsion, it is only for the lost.

I allowed myself to be lost in her grasp, her call, that one on the telephone, that one that kept me returning to Asia. I guess it was the same one that allowed this addition to wreak havoc upon my soul and keep me coming back for more.

Her eyes they were dark, they looked down upon me with the purest source of love that she could muster up. An embrace followed, encountered by another. I continued to stare, with all my self-disgust, into the space of nothing and no return.

Here I was again trapped, held, bound to the world of the love of no love, the feeling, in a person who does not know what it means to feel. I wanted to be elsewhere doing other things than simply wasting my aging time with a person who I had known all her intimacies in a pervious existence, a pervious lifetime and had run from them before.

Now here I was being kissed, kissing back and once again, as before hating myself for it and crying to the highest god to find me a way out, to a world where I choose to dwell where illusion was far closer at hand and its price not so high.

That, like that of the notes out of the mouth of a gothic opera singer, I was attacked again, forced back into the realms of pagan reality, it was not the looking around, it was instead the feeling around, I was hit by The Heat.

*   *   *

some worlds have reason
some whys have none
lost between the two
lost in-between the desire for existence
and knowing that this world
must have something more to offer
addiction takes hold
compulsion never lets you go
extremes
in a path
that clings only to the middle way
the main streams
I cling to the extremes
I long for the extremes
I exist in the extremes
I walk their razors edge
it kills me further
each step
that I take

*   *   *

Some how age was taking its toll upon me that morning. Lust, lost desire, name it what you will, the pup, my weed did not care for action. My mind, instead lost in the dilemmas of the encroaching real world. Money, fame, and being somewhere other than where and what I was, or should I say was and was not.

Once, I was maybe nineteen years old, I lived in this apartment building out in the Val of L.A. A lot of party youngsters inhabited its walls. I was this pseudo yogi living on the fringes, lost between celibacy and rock and roll. My clothing was East Indian, those around me, denim.

Up the stairs, for you see I lived on the second floor, in this little single, complete with cockroaches, of a two-floor building constructed in the 1960's. Across the stairwell lived this one bad dude, mustache in hand. His babe had apparently dumped him and being one of those dudes with feelings, it kind of kicked him over the deep end. I made a comment to this N Y out to the coast homeboy of mine, who eventually shacked up in this guys crib,

"Man, that guy should have his life together by twenty seven."
"You can't say that man, you just can't say that."

At the time, I thought that I could, 'say that.' As the years had passed though, my life had defiantly not taken the course that I had hoped of, dreamed of, planned for. So, there I was approaching thirty in the fast lane, no fame, no fortune, no money, not even being the forever lifetime monk which I had planned to be once upon a younger time.

I understood what the dude, at the ripe old age of twenty-three, had meant. Where had his wisdom come from?

*   *   *

Enough with the distraction, I should get on with the story.

"Can we just end this thing now, before it begins again?"

I asked the question with the actually hopes that the response may be affirmative but in my heart I knew that there was no chance of that.

"You are always looking for a way out."
"You are always running away."
"Have you always been like this?"

The same questions, the same connotations, I had heard them all before from those very same lips. It touched a bad spot in me. I felt trapped, tied and when I feel that I generally want to fight my way out.

I stood up in all of my naked glory. I didn't want to talk; I did not wish to be in this/that situation. The walls they looked closer, the room smaller, and The Heat hotter.

I proceeded to dress myself. My last love, (well, love as much as I can), it was the same story, you know. One would think that I would have learned my lesson. Not returned into a semi-situation that took control of all my time, that grabbed my soul by the balls.

I felt it even than, the first moments back together, the pressure, taken from my creativity, taken from my illusion, that of which that I actually had something to offer the world. I was the fool, she was the fool, both believing that there was something more, and the possibility of, going on more than there was.

The Roll

Damn, I have been on one hell of a roll. It all started, I guess, about two, well no now going on about three weeks ago. I mean it has been pumping. But with that comes all of the artistic frustration of one too many babes, and one too many places to be to be sitting here at the typing keys and recording it for the living literature of the late twentieth century. You know, like that is all the paradox of the whole thing. You have got to live/experience to have anything to create at all but then when it gets moving there is no time to do the above said.

I don't know, it seems/I guess that my life has always been like this, either full power on or zero nada. Well, for whatever it is worth, there is the two sides of the state of mind and now if I may, like you know, roll on into the storyline.

Venchenzo had this vacation coming up, I knew because we had done a little family (his) session over at his bros Saturday Jims crib of matrimony back a bit. A bit before this all went down and got underway. Well, I'm a godfather so I guess I'm linked up in that family thAng too.

Saturday Jim chilling on the party side of things these days, you know like getting way domestic: now hides all the serious boos, and tells me, "Big guy, don't get on a roll." The time was when he would party as hard, if not harder than everyone. The times they are a changing. To each their own.

It always kind of bother me his approach to his technique though. Like before he got latched up he would tell me what a wimp I was when ever I would have a babe on the line and do all he could to bring me out to the night. As you may now know, me, I would usually go. But when it came down to him, it way far no-go, "Like I can not man." When I would later bust him on this fact, he would just give me the "I know." Like what the fuck does that mean?

Anyway so now he is in to the no drink mode now and gives the eye of put down whenever any one else is. Well that is AOK too, that is just him. But it always just strikes me funny, how people get holy somewhere down the line. Me, sometimes I climb on the wagon and don't drink too. If they do AOK. But anyway, just for the record here, I am not being hypocritical here I have laid all this SJ's direction.

But the whole party went down, and I got kind of the negative vibes from the family who don't understand me not being married, not having a job, and blaming me for all of the problems of their children, bad influence and all. But basically I do not believe in bad and good. And if you want to call the truth, they did way more in my younger years to influence me into the world of the drink. So what ever all of this is worth, just an artist using his method to like cry out his dilemmas, I guess.

Anyway Venchenzo needed a ride home, when I offered, it was full on smiles for he knew the night was young, and the party it was at hand.

We bail over his cribs direction and change up into more appropriate attire. We grab the old local underground paper, look for an appropriate club. We find one, we go.

Now you know, I don't know if I have ever told you about it but the L.A. club scene has changed. There was a time back in the punk days, when Venchenzo and I reigned supreme, but... nothing lasts forever. So now, the almost disco, funk dance clubs, walls naturally painted black, are in control. You know with all the hip and trendy, no real purpose people, frequenting them. Oh yes and of course with a price tag to match.

Anyway inside we strut, just to set the scene. We grabbed a couple of mineral water, Venchenzo had just recently picked up a duce post falling asleep at the wheel, crashing his brand new Stang, after drinking all night and then running into some cars, well a lot of cars. So he was in the program and they may give him periotic tests, so he chilled back. AOK, I can drink the bad brew mineral water myself.

A funny little story here, if I may. I guess it must be three, maybe four years back. Venchenzo, I, and this other homeboy we be out gothic rocking, once upon a time. We did the after hours club and the etcetera. Well to make a long story short, we were fucked up. Anyway Venchenzo behind the wheel going home down the freeway, you know. I look over and the bad homeboy his head is down and he is asleep, "Wake up!" "Oh, OK man, I'm not sleeping." I look again and he is nodded, this time about to run into the car passing us on the side. Well, as you can see he does have the tendency to be asleep at the wheel.

We stood around, scooped the place, it was boppin' but, I don't know, not really our scene. We moved over to one side, caught another bad mineral water and up comes this chick and asks me to dance. She had a friend with her so I told Venchenzo to go for it. He moved but it was no-go. I guess it was all his hair. These babes must dig it long like mine. And with the get with the program, and have to do a few serious session in court old Venchenzo had wacked his long hair GI style, so…

I danced on for a few, then we left the floor. The chick obviously wanted to rap and have me buy her a drink. But how should I say, she was only so-so, so chill factor zero in the drink department, and the night it was young...

Cruised up next to Venchenzo now sitting to the side with a mineral water in his hand. We stared into the abyss. Down below, on the first level, of these black carpeted two level bleacher style seats, sat this babe brushing out her hair. I decide well the best thing is to help her on out so I began to run my hand along it and she just keeps on, keeping on. Venchenzo gives me the thumbs up.

Well, I don't know, I'm going to give it to you straight and simple, let's keep it to one paragraph. She was a semi dog. I had Venchenzo buy her a drink. She had three very serious babes of friends, which whom I must admit I did dance a few with. One was twenty-eight, younger then me but looked thirty-five; she was married, two of the little ones. The sister, babe city, twenty-two, looked thirty, this was

---

113

her bachelorette party. Other friend, twenty-three, looked it, was engaged. The ugly one wanted to bail with big V. and me and get boned. Post the dancing, 3:00 AM, we just walked on, our dicks in our hands, into the sun rise.

That was that, but that was the beginning. Venchenzo didn't make it to his hundred and fifty hours of community service the next day, cleaning graffiti off of the walls, but he had a vacation coming up the next week, so the preverbal stage was set.

Monday night a local banger club. A local friend's band to see. I strutted solo in, left with a thin, booted, and leathered banger chick. I banged her but the sitch, nothing for the record books; zero in a zero world.

Tuesday night, I give him, Venchenzo, the little ring on the telephone, time for this little private club on the Hollywood head banger side of the picture where the stars come out to play, and oh yes meat is available and way far easy to come by.

We cruised in. We drank mineral water. Venchenzo felt a bit naked with out his hair. I too have known the feeling.

We latched up with more then a babe or three. One even, as I walked past, had to lay her hands on my wild sex machine, giving it a bit of the may-sage. She was ugly, later baby. I even laid my number in the Asian direction of this one babe, "She will call within the week."

We actually bumped, I mean banged into this babe a few stories back, the party one who wanted to come down and listen to my record collection, you know. She was there too. I just put the chill, not interested on her, she caught the vibes.

So we fractured our ear drums a bit to a live band. Venchenzo even hit the dance floor with this one babe. Me, I stood there a-rap'n to her soul sister of a friend. Never did understand how you can dance to that type of music.

We bailed the door, with them. The night it was getting old. Soul mom was up for the ride to a late night dinner spot. Whity was not. We went home alone but the movement it had been placed in motion, and the dance it was at hand.

Come Thursday Venchenzo needed another car, for as mentioned his ride was in the full on tattered condition. He had originally planned to pick up a scoot, (a motor-cycle). Me, I planned to take out life insurance on him if he did for I gave him a few months to live. The boy does like to party you know. So we went out and looked at a few, '65, '66 Stangs. Not new, like his other/last one but badassed, just the same.

A session here, session there

Wo' Ton of the Blue Vision

I had spent a restless summer bound by the boundaries of L.A. With little money in pockets, and/or bank accounts, diversion was needed but not so easily obtainable. My life, my path, if you will, has always lead me a bit to the side of the mainstream, thus, traditional employment was never my game-plan. I was admittedly a bit lost.

With the particulars and introductions out of the way, on to the story...

I had awoken from a dream, into the warming temperatures of an early afternoon day. The dream had taken to me a grotto type place where this spiritual teacher was given a discourse. The lady, upon waking I indeed knew, she was a Western person who had been given the roll of leading this large spiritual group, once the India born guru had left his body many years the previous. Though I knew of the lady, and of the teachings of the group, personally I had never pressured their knowledge, though as a young spiritual aspirant I had studied their teachings.

Awoken, from this very vivid dream, unable to forget it, and having, as my lifestyle demonstrated, no better place to be, I decided to travel on to their center on Sunset Blvd. and just see where this dream may lead…

Upon arrival, I strolled around the beautiful ground, to get into the vibes of the place if you will. Then I proceeded into the bookstore where I hope to find deeper realizations into the propensities of my dream.

I ask as to this ladies coming plans and was quite surprisingly informed that she was to give a public lecture this coming Sunday. As I was not an initiate of the sect I inquired as to my ability to attend. It was checked into, and after a bit of this and a tad of that, it was confirmed that yes, I could attend. Well…

So, I spent the rest of that day and the next few days doing my tradition this and that and then Sunday came. Into my van I got and I drove to the downtown location where the lecture was to be given. Parking always being a problem down there I played around a bit and then found this underground garage where I puled in. I was however, informed that they did not allow vans to park in there. Stupid I thought, I mean if my van fit, which it did not always do, I mean why not. But this argument did not hold much validity with the imported from Mexico, parking attendant, so… Out I pulled.

Around the side, over to one side of this large old brick building where I was to attend the lecture I found this abandoned parking lot and though I was sure it was no-go to park there, it was after all Sunday so… I decided to go for it anyway.

I walked around and made my way into this building I had seen millions of times but had never really gone into. In the main lobby, I was greeted by quite a surprise; a million people waiting in line to get in to see this lady.

Now, I don't really know what it was, for it was not something which I really planned to do, but I just began to proceed along the line, looking and smiling at the occasional face which I recognized; you know, its a small world, in any circle, spiritual or otherwise. I got to the head of the line and I just walked into the auditorium where she was to give her talk. Once inside, I could see that it was almost completely full. I guess it was not anticipated that so many would attend but I found one of the last seats available and sat down into the almost stifling due to lack of air and almost claustrophobic atmosphere due to the amount of people.

I sat there wondering, questioning what had led me to this place, was I to have some deep spiritual realization? I sat there; the time quickly was upon me when she walked out.

Yes, she did have quite a pure aura about her, simple and kind. She began to lecture.

As I write these pages now, I do not even remember what she spoke of. It seems that all spiritual teachers say the same thing from a different point of view, yes?

The time went on, the words went on, perhaps a half hour or so into the lecture, I got up and left. Why? I was not quite sure. It just seem that the lack of oxygen, the amount of people who were so blindly listening to her words, their so knowing blank stares, like they knew they were drinking spiritual elixir. I don't know, I was changing, and this type of mindless devotion was just something which I had seeming left behind, long ago, after leaving India. There was nothing there for me.

I walked down the long corridor, where people still waited to enter. Well, at least one more person would be able to see her holy form. I exited.

There is this park, Pershing Square as it is called, across the street from the building I was in. I, quite dumbfounded as to why I had this dream only to be 'turned off' by the whole event decided I would walk over there and ponder all of this reality.

The air was fairly cool outside this day; almost overcast. There was the traditional bum or thirty who hit me up for some change but in all honesty, I had none to slice them up.

There was a bench in which no one was inhabiting, so I pulled up a seat and lost myself into the realms of ponder. Why...

I looked to the sky, watched some birds as they passed, studied the noise of the city streets as the cars, as the people passed; nothing, I had no answers. A mother, Latin, pushing her small child in a carriage passed me. The child full of stares, lost into my form. I looked back at the lad, nothing to offer but my smile. They walked on, I thought on.

What had led me to this place, why? The eternal question, why...

As I was sitting, in actuality about ready to leave, up comes this man; fairly dark skinned, maybe forty years old: wore jeans, a blue cotton shirt. If it was not for the long length of his hair, which was quite long and worn in a pony tail, I would have thought him to probably be of Mexican origin. As in this area, many Mexican born people frequented. Well, I mean, after all Los Angeles, once did belong to Mexico... 'El Pueblo de Nuestra Señora la REINA DE LOS ÁNGELES'

He came up, sat down on my bench, said, "Hello, nice day isn't it."